This special signed
edition is limited to
1000 numbered copies
and 26 lettered copies.

This is copy ___836___ .

ROBERT JACKSON BENNETT

IN THE
SHADOWS
OF MEN

ROBERT JACKSON BENNETT

Subterranean Press
2020

First Edition

ISBN
978-1-59606-987-9

Subterranean Press
PO Box 190106
Burton, MI 48519

subterraneanpress.com

Manufactured in the United States of America

T O TRAVEL ACROSS WEST TEXAS at night is to pass through bursts of bright and seas of shadow, these sudden punctuations of towns clinging to the highways as they slash through the scrub. It is a place of tremendous opposites and inverses. An aging, unlit asphalt road will suddenly flow into a smooth, cement highway, fresh and new and lit up white. Then you will pass through countless tiny villages that are seemingly abandoned, all crumbling grain silos and mid-century town squares with the shopfronts boarded up, only to find the city at the next intersection is a booming hive, its gas stations fresh and new and crowded with muddy men in square-toed boots.

To travel through west Texas is to travel through a strikingly bipolar place, an empty land that has somehow gone mad overnight, suddenly teeming with trucks and truckers and workers and trailers as dozens of companies converge on the desert flats to plumb the depths of the Permian. You don't grasp the whole of it until you come to the frack sites themselves and see the gas burning, these giant, coiling flares unscrolling from the towers, whipping in the wind like brilliant windsocks. The light is so bright, flooding the landscape around the towers for hundreds of yards, making the many shadows dance like witches in the woods.

You see one flare, and then another, and another. Then dozens of them, hundreds of them. A land studded with giant candles burning in the darkness, apparently unobserved, unwatched. As I drive through the frack sites I am reminded of votive candles flickering in a devotional. Yet the flares are curiously greasy at the ends, I find, an oily, unpleasant glimmer—a reminder, perhaps, that what is being burned has spent millions of years sleeping miles and miles under the skin of the earth.

It was here long before we came, but in a handful of years we will eliminate this curious geological phenomenon. We will drain it dry and we will burn it up and then move on.

These sites are the finished places, the sites where the work has been done. At the unfinished places you see the man-camps, the fleets and fleets of trailers and trucks where the roughnecks and the construction workers and the sand haulers sleep. A curious herd of men, migratory and nomadic, slipping from desert site to desert site bringing their water and electricity and creature comforts with them.

They are here, of course, for the same reason I am here, for the same reason all of us are here: to make money. We are here to wring money from the sands and stones of this unforgiving place. And I mean to do it.

WHEN I FINALLY FIND THE town of Coahora it is like many in this part of the world, half-heartedly clinging to the highway, about ready to give up and recede into the red earth. The town itself feels abandoned in the night. I cannot imagine people living here.

I drive around it to the northern point, glimpsing a streak of modern highway in the distance, cold and white. It is busy with traffic, but the only thing Coahora gets is the faint sound of tires.

I drive farther north, squinting at the white screen of my phone. I continue until I spy an old gravel road at the base of the streetlight, heading east into the scrub. I turn, and the road leads me up a very slight slope.

A pair of headlights flashes on in the darkness, still and stationary. There's the honk of a horn. I point my truck at the lights and accelerate.

As I approach I see a building at the top of the hill: an old motel, built in a large, square U. I can tell at a glance that it was built in the sixties or seventies—its roof is just peaky in that kind of way. There is a tall signpost out front, but the words are faded and the paint is gone. The sign looks to have been made in the shape of a crescent moon.

An F-150 is parked before the motel's check-in office, the lights on, the engine off. A man is sitting on the hood, bent over the light of his phone. I park, get out, and walk over to him.

It is as I approach that I realize I have not spoken to another human soul in over two weeks. It is suddenly strange to do so now, alone in the dark of west Texas with this aged motel reaching out to me. But that is why I did this. I was stuck in Houston, trapped and alone and frozen. So when my brother reached out to me with this curious job offer on the outskirts of Coahora, I accepted, if only to break the silence.

"Hey, Bear," I say as I walk up.

"A hundred and fifty thousand," says my brother. He does not look up from his phone.

"What?"

"A hundred and fifty thousand goddamn dollars. Guess who is making a hundred and fifty thousand goddamn dollars in Pecos, just thirty minutes away."

"I don't know. Who?"

"Barbers. *Barbers.* Fuckers who cut hair all day! And you know why?"

"No."

"Because these goddamn roughnecks got no one else to go to. Hell, if it was me, I'd buy some clippers and just shave my head. Save me some money." He jumps off the hood of the truck and looks at me. "How you doing, little brother?"

We embrace. "I'm okay," I say.

"Yeah?"

"Yeah."

"Well, it's a hell of a trip, I'll say that."

I study my brother as he releases me. He looks good: his body is filled out, his beard is full, his hair long. His teeth, I note with care, are clean, and he is not jittering or shaking.

I was somewhat worried. Addicts such as he are prone to taking up projects obsessively only to abandon them halfway through, and this endeavor offers no end of projects.

But he looks clean. He looks whole. I know what Bear looks like when he's using, and it is not this.

I look at the motel beyond. Its doors are shut, its windows dark. "This is it, huh."

"Yeah, that's it. That's our goldmine." He paces along the line of closed doors. "They got motel rooms going for seven hundred dollars a night in Midland. We ain't in the heart of it, but it's close enough to I-20 that we'll still catch more than enough business. Especially those boys that don't have their own trailers and RVs and shit."

I nod at the faded sign, carved in a crescent moon. "What was it called?"

"Huh? Oh. The Moon and Stars Motel. Dumbass name, really. I sure as shit ain't calling it that."

We walk along the face of the motel, peering through the darkened windows. "How many rooms?" I ask.

"Forty. It's a big half-circle, twenty rooms on either side, with the office in the middle. I got here about an hour ago, just kind of poked around, but it's in fine shape, really, considering it hasn't had a guest in about ten years." He jangles a set of keys. "Let's take a look."

We walk up to the check-in office. There's a transaction window facing the parking lot, one of those windows with the speaker and the slot at the bottom where people can slide over cash or checks. Bear opens the office door and turns on the flashlight on his phone and we peer around.

The office appears to have held up well. It is quite small, but it has no mold, though it's dusty and crackling in places. The walls are wood-paneled—very mid-century—and a tall, built-in desk fills up half the room. A metal bell sits at the edge of the desk, ancient and covered in dust. Bear walks up to it and slaps the button with his palm. It makes a sad little *plonk* noise.

"Yeah, this'll do fine," he says. He walks to one wall and taps at a wood panel. It falls off and crackles to pieces on the linoleum floor. "The superficial stuff wasn't well built, but that doesn't matter. We can gut all this shit and the rest of the rooms in no time. Doesn't need to be fancy, just serviceable."

I walk up to the desk and look at the setup. A rolling chair is still parked behind it, its red leather a dull brown behind countless years of dust. It sits facing the transaction window like it's still awaiting a customer. "Who owned this place, again?"

"An uncle of Dad's. Guy named Corbin Pugh. Never heard of him myself."

I have not either. I know very little about our father, or his side of the family. He left when I was very small. Though I just assume my father is now dead, I have no way to know even that.

"How much did it set you back?" I ask.

"Five grand. It went to some cousin of ours, and he sold it to me for peanuts. He didn't want to bother with it and he didn't know how valuable it could be. This was a hopping place back in the seventies, back during the last oil boom. It can hop again. I bet we can turn it around before spring. I'll cut you in for thirty for your work, little brother. I'd do half, but I can't afford it, so for now it'll have to be thirty."

I nod.

"That okay?"

"Yes."

"You don't want to negotiate?"

I shrug. "No?"

He looks at me carefully. "Okay. Hop back in your truck. The main house is around back."

"Main house?"

"Where Corbin lived. We can stay there while we work on the motel."

I GET IN MY TRUCK and he gets in his, and I follow him around the side of the motel to where a small gravel road leads away into the desert. The night is full dark and all I can see is what my headlights show me, which is not much. Eventually they flash upon an old one-story house on the hill behind the motel, a ranch style build that was popular in the sixties. My brother's arm emerges from the driver side window of his truck and he points to where I need to park.

"I poked around here a bit," says Bear as he jumps out of his truck. He grabs a duffel bag and throws it over his shoulder. "City hasn't turned on the water, so that's going to suck for a bit, but the walls are standing and it's warm. Still has some of the old man's shit from when he died. No beds, though."

I follow him to the side door and he fumbles with his keys. He looks at me over his shoulder. "Ain't you gonna get your shit?"

"Oh. I don't have any."

"You didn't pack?"

I shrug.

"Goddamn, boy," he says, and he shakes his head and opens the door.

We stalk in through a narrow, dark hallway. Bear flicks a switch and a flat, greasy light flutters to life in the darkness, revealing a linoleum-floored kitchen and peeling cupboards and cabinets.

I look around. A shabby easy chair sits facing a giant, ancient television that must weigh at least a hundred pounds. There are ghostly marks on the walls from where pictures once hung, but only one is left: an old print depicting the battle of San Jacinto, with the name and the date below it. The blinds still dangle from a few windows, their slats closed. Somehow the interior feels like it has only been a week or so since the previous owner lived here—it has that kind of recent stillness to it, like I could press a hand to the seat of the easy chair and find it warm.

"I'll buy water from the Dollar Store in Pecos," says my brother, throwing down his duffel bag. "We can make do while we figure out the scope of work. I brought a grill and a cooler, figure we can bust it out tonight."

Dinner is sausages cooked on the Weber grill on the patio. We sit in lawn chairs out back under the crumbling patio roof, our breath frosting in the cold air, and we drink air-cooled beer and stare at the starlit desolation beyond the house, pale and fragile and empty.

"So you own this whole property?" I ask him.

"Proud owner of six acres of nothing."

I watch as the wind batters the frail scrub. "It's something."

Bear spits on the ground. "It's a shithole. I just plan to try to make a buck off it. You'd have to be a miserable son of a bitch to live your whole life out here, and I guess Corbin was a miserable shit, to hear Dad talk about this place."

"Dad talked about this place?"

"Yeah. Said he had to work a summer or two here once. Maybe old Corbin Pugh was one son of a bitch to work for. Which makes sense. Since Dad was a son of a bitch."

There is a silence.

"I'm not surprised you don't remember Dad talking about it," says Bear. "When did they pull you out?"

"I think I was five."

My brother considers the beer in his hand. His eyes sit small and shrewd within his skull. "Lucky boy," he says. "How's your little girl?"

"Fat and loud."

"That's good. When'd you see her last?"

"Week or two ago."

"When Alice left?"

I nod.

"Shit. Sounds like it was a hell of a thing."

"It was."

"You want to talk about it?"

"No," I say.

He studies me, leaning forward to peer into my face. It is an achingly familiar gesture, one I remember instantly from my childhood: Bear examining my face, my neck, my shoulders, trying to take scope of the damage. "You sure?" he says.

I shrug. What is there to say?

"Living," Bear pronounces, "is a hell of a lot harder than people let on. Come on. Let's get to bed. We got shit to do tomorrow."

We go inside and he unpacks two sleeping bags. "I figured it'd be best to prepare. Carpet's dusty but at least it's soft."

I tell him I will make do. I am drunk and I am tired and I have seen too many headlights in the darkness. I unzip the sleeping bag and stuff myself inside and shut my eyes.

Then I hear his voice in the dark: "The Oasis," he says.

"What?" I say.

"The Oasis. That's what I'm thinking about calling it. The motel."

It takes me a second to process this. "Oh."

"You like it?"

"I like it."

"Good. I like it. I like it, too."

IT IS IN THE NIGHT that I hear it—the sounds of movement in the hallway, the carpet being crushed underfoot with step after step. I open my eyes but it's so dark that I can see little of the empty room around—we are too far from civilization to catch the luminescence from a streetlight.

But I think I can see the doorway. I listen to the footsteps, woozy and half-dreaming, and watch as someone comes to the door and looks in at me. A male figure, tall and broad, wearing a white crew-cut T-shirt, his face lost in darkness. In the shadows of the hallway he is little more than a fading imprint of a man.

"Bear?" I ask.

The man looks at me for a moment longer, then slowly turns and lumbers away.

"Bear?" I ask again.

There is no answer.

I go to my brother's room and find him snoring in his sleeping bag. The hallway is empty, as is the living room and kitchen. The doors are locked tight.

Troubled, I go back to bed. I must sleep. For we have work tomorrow.

WE START WITH THE ROOF.

It's been a long time since I did roof work on a house, but I find I have not missed it. Bear has rented a dumpster and we spend three days ripping off the crumbling asphalt shingles and tossing them over the edge of the roof. The sheathing under them is rotted so that needs replacing, and then that means we need an ice guard membrane, and then more asphalt roofing paper, and drip edging—and on, and on, and on.

"Fuck howdy," says Bear as we begin nailing the shingles down, starting at the eaves and working toward the peaks. "They sure as shit had a lot of goddamn peaks back then."

It takes a week and a half—eleven days of toil and constantly driving one, two, three towns away to get more materials—but finally we finish the roof. I did not expect this work to be glamorous but I am a bit surprised by how filthy and uncivilized we become. It takes the city three days to turn our water on, which means we have no showers or baths for much of this work. Even when the water is turned on, the washer and dryer still don't work and we do not have time to purchase new ones, so we wash our clothes with detergent in buckets and hang them out to dry in the house, as the dust from the wind would make them unusable in minutes if we hung them outside.

"I'll get one of those commercial grade washer and dryers," says Bear as he pins his underwear up in the bedroom and turns on the ceiling fan. "Install it at the motel. And then I'll never have to do this fucking shit again."

Once the roof is done we start the demolition, donning our masks and ripping out the brittle, crackling, built-in furniture and the crumbling drywall. It is cheap stuff, all built at least two or three decades ago. We make trip after trip, hauling splintering wood or dragging mattresses across the asphalt to the dumpster.

The days slip by one after another, a haze of dust and drywall and particle board. We talk little—neither of us were ever talkers—but I suspect Bear has troubles on his mind he does not wish to give voice to. After all, I know I have my own.

I TRY NOT TO COUNT, but you can't, not really. The days are etched into the underside of all my thoughts.

It has been thirty-nine days. Thirty-nine days since I walked away from my job installing windows because I could not stop thinking about picking up a hammer and driving it into my boss's skull. Thirty-nine days since my wife left and she packed our little girl into her car and said she couldn't stand it anymore, she just wanted to go someplace where everything wasn't ugly all the time.

And then I was just alone. And I stayed in the house, waiting, sleeping, not speaking, not sure what to do, until finally my phone rang and I picked up to hear Bear on the other end, and I jumped in my truck and just left, because leaving was all there was to do.

I am not sure where my wife and daughter are now. At her parents' house, I suspect. I wonder how they sleep and what they do. I wonder what I would say to them now, or how to talk to them at all, how to be the thing they needed or expected me to be.

This was not how it was supposed to go, I think as I toss another armful of ancient wood into the dumpster. This was not the story I was supposed to live. I was supposed to get a job and a wife and a child and we were supposed to flourish. It was not supposed to be so hard to do every little thing, to handle the bills and the feedings and the daycare and the payments and the work, always the work.

It was not supposed to be like this. Nothing was supposed to be like this. Everything was not supposed to be so goddamned hard.

WE COMPLETE ONE HALF OF the rooms, then move to the check-in office. We pry all the paneled wood from the walls—it comes off practically just when you glance at it—and then set about removing the built-in desk.

"I like that chair," said Bear. He nods at the red-leather rolling chair behind the desk. "We'll keep that. Move it up to the house."

"But bust up the rest?"

"Yeah." Bear walks around and pulls out a drawer. "Shit. Guess we'll have to empty all this."

As he pulls out more drawers I walk around to take a look. I see they are full of ancient, brittle paper and pens that must be at least twenty or thirty years old by now. Guest registration forms so faded they're like ghosts of papers. Heaps and heaps of tattered stationery.

"Dump them," says Bear, and he pulls one drawer out and takes it outside to the dumpster.

I do the same, and we create a train, walking back and forth. It's on the third trip out that I notice something in one of the drawers.

I pause and slowly put the drawer down on the asphalt, peering inside. The front half is papers and receipt stock and the like—but the back half is full of Polaroid pictures, all packed together with rubber bands. I kneel and pick up one of the stacks of pictures—the rubber band crumbles the instant I touch it—and I leaf through them.

Most of the pictures are so aged and faded that I can't make them out. But some are still clear—and, most curiously, they depict the same thing every time: the sliding window of the office check-in, viewed from within the office, looking out at the parking lot.

In each picture the transaction window is open, and a person is peering in.

I flip through the pictures, one after another. The people in the window are different in each picture: a different face at a different time of day and, going by their clothing, the years are different as well. Some were taken in the 1970s, I suspect, while others were in the eighties. The people are all posing for their photographs, some grudgingly, others with beaming smiles on their faces, like models at an art shoot.

As I keep looking through the pictures, I realize the people in the window are all women, and all fairly young. Many are Mexican, or Mexican-looking. Not a single man is among them.

"What you got?" calls Bear as he returns from the dumpster.

"Come see this."

Bear looks at the pictures with me, shuffling through them one after the other. There has be at least thirty of them, not even counting the faded ones. The regularity of the positioning—a face in a frame, always taken from behind the check-in desk—makes me think of mug shots at a police station.

"You think Corbin Pugh took these?" I ask.

"I guess. Don't know who else would."

"So—he took pictures of the lady guests?"

"Can't imagine they'd tolerate that," he says. "That'd be weird as hell."

"Maybe he knew them, then?"

Bear doesn't respond. He has pulled out one picture and is staring at it. He turns the picture around. "Guess this was him."

This picture is not a Polaroid. It is quite old, perhaps forty or fifty years old. It shows a tall, towering slab of a man standing by a woman in front of a brick wall. Neither of them are smiling. The man is wearing a crew-neck white T-shirt with black slacks. His hair is styled in a sloppy pompadour, like someone trying to emulate Johnny Cash but unwilling to put in the work to really pull it off. His nose is broad, his eyes wide and shallow, his neck so thick he almost has no chin.

He looks, in other words, a lot like a Pugh—a lot like my father, or the memories I have of my father from when I was small. And a lot like me and Bear.

"Damn," I say.

"Yeah. The family resemblance is pretty goddamned striking, if you ask me."

I look at the woman standing beside him, her arms crossed, her back stooped. Either she is very small, or he is very big—though I suspect it to be the latter. She is a dainty creature, with large eyes and a wide mouth and a curiously square upper lip. Her straight brown hair is parted down the middle. Somehow her waifish features give her a constant look of constant, dispirited surprise.

"What a happy couple," said Bear. "Dump it. I'll get the sledges and axes."

I take the drawer over to the dumpster, and I toss it and its contents in. But I keep the picture of Corbin Pugh and the small woman, sliding it into my pocket.

I am not sure why I do this, even as I do it. There is something so striking about the image of Corbin Pugh that it's like a bell was rung in the recesses of my head. Part of it is just how much he looked like my father, but another part of it is his size, and how he stands. It is familiar to me.

I think of the man I imagined in the house that night, now two weeks ago, standing in my doorway. Tall and broad in a crew-neck T-shirt.

I wonder. But I do not wonder for long. Because then we find the door.

WE MOVE ON TO THE far leg of the U shape of the motel. By this time we have demolished twenty guest rooms, so we have a system down, ripping out the built-in furniture, hauling out the drywall, leaving only the plumbing and the linoleum flooring to tackle later. But it is as I pull out the remains of the built-in bed that I find something I did not expect.

There is a glint of metal in the corner. Right where a small, red easy chair had sat previously.

I pause, walk over, stoop, and look at it. It is an electrical socket, mounted in the floor—but none of the other rooms had one of these. All their sockets were wall sockets.

Then I spy something else, close to the socket in the linoleum floor. At first it almost appears to be a little metal caterpillar crawling across the linoleum—but then I realize it is a hinge, like that of a door or a window shutter. And after a moment of searching, I find a second hinge in the floor, about three feet above that.

And where there are hinges, I know there must be a door.

I shake one glove off and run my hand over the flooring. I find a crack in the linoleum, small but straight, running from hinge to hinge. The crack marches in a square across the floor, and it runs directly through the electrical socket.

I look at the socket, screwed in by one Phillips-head screw. I take out my screwdriver, unscrew it, and pry the metal plate away.

Below the plate is no electrical wiring of any kind. Rather, there is a small handle. The entire electrical socket, it seems, was built to hide this.

Bear walks into the room. "What you looking at?" he asks.

I do not answer. I stand, grab the handle, and pull.

"Huh?" he says. "Whoa—what the hell?"

The panel of flooring swings up. It sends a giant cloud of dust billowing around me. I wave it away, and my brother comes to stand beside me, and we stare down at what lies below.

There is a hatch door in the foundation underneath the floor. It is made of steel, like the door of a bank vault, and it is big enough for a man to slip though. A tumbling combination lock is installed above its handle, awaiting four numbers. Currently it is set to 1946.

We stare at the hatch in silence. Then Bear reaches down, grabs it by the handle, and gives it a pull. It does not move.

"Well," he says, sounding resigned. "What the fuck."

"What is this thing?" I ask.

He idly tries a few combinations, but the hatch refuses to give. "It must run down into the goddamn foundation."

"Is it a bomb shelter?"

"I don't know. Guess it looks like it."

"Why would he build a bomb shelter into one of his guest rooms?"

"Hell, I don't know. In case a goddamn bomb fell, I guess." He kicks the door. It is so solid it does not echo or reverberate. "All's I know is we're not getting through that door anytime soon. Not without a torch to burn the damn lock out."

There is a silence as we stare at the hatch.

"So what do we do?" I ask.

"What do you mean, what do we do?"

"I mean, do we go rent a torch and burn through it?"

"Hell no. We don't have time for that. So. One of the rooms has a goddamn trapdoor in it. So what? We'll just, I don't know, put a rug over it or something. Or we just won't rent out this room."

I study the steel hatch, examining the frame, the jamb. It's expert work, carefully crafted. "What exactly do we know about Corbin Pugh, again?"

"What? Nothing except that he was an asshole."

I keep studying the hatch, frowning.

"We'll just ignore it, okay?" he says. "Goddamn! We just got to have this place running for a year or two to make our buck off of it." He shuts the linoleum trapdoor, replaces the electrical socket plate, and screws it back in. "We'll just stick something on top of the goddamn thing and forget about it. Come on. We've got more rooms to do and I've only got the dumpster for a little while longer. Let's get a move on."

We depart, but I can tell that he is as troubled by this secret door as I am. It is then that I begin to wonder what else might be hiding on the property.

THAT NIGHT WE EAT AGAIN on the patio, huddled about the Weber grill. This time it's hamburgers, and Bear dances the meat around on the grill, avoiding the flash of flaming grease. It is a clear night, bright and cold, and in the starlight the ragged landscape looks like an inversion of itself, like the world's been flipped inside out.

We sit on the folded chairs, quietly eating. I keep thinking about the hatch in the guest room, wondering which four numbers could unlock it—and then, once it was unlocked, what I might find below.

Then there is a quiet buzz, and I jump, surprised. It takes me a moment to realize my phone has just vibrated.

"What's up?" says Bear.

I pull out my phone. Reception in this desolate place is surprisingly excellent—the fracking industry has brought many things to west Texas, including decent coverage—but I've yet to have any contact with the outside world.

It's a text message. I peer at it. It is from my wife.

I read it. I read it again, and again.

"What's up?" says Bear again.

"Message from Alice," I say. I find I feel very numb. "I need to go back to Houston."

"For what?"

"To transfer the car title over to her."

"Shit," says Bear. He sits back. "You guys really splitting up, you think?"

"I don't know."

"Have you talked about it?"

"Haven't talked about much."

"Well. Do you want to?"

I sit in silence.

"Shit," he says again. "Well. I know it was never for me, brother. Never bothered trying my hand at marriage, or living with someone. I knew from the get-go I wasn't going to be a fast hand at that. Maybe you and me just aren't made for civilized living."

I stare at the phone in my hand. I could have talked to her, I realize, told her what I was doing, where I'd gone. But I know then that I have said nothing and done nothing because I knew this would happen. It was like a bubble—to touch it would mean it would pop, and then this part of my life would truly be over and gone and lost, forever.

But perhaps it was already lost. Perhaps I knew that, too.

Suddenly Bear sits up, staring out at the empty land behind the house. "What the hell," he says.

"What is it?" I say.

He leans forward, eyes narrow, mouth agape in shock. "Who in the hell is that?"

I look out at the scrub behind the house. The sand and rock and mesquite trees seem spectral and pale in the moonlight, but I can see no one. "Who's who?"

"That guy. That guy just walking around out there. Right there."

Bear points, and I think I can see where he is pointing to—a clearing in the mesquite trees—but I can't spy anyone out there. The night is dark and still and silent.

"Who?" I say.

"Son of a bitch!" says Bear. He stands and runs into the house.

"Bear?" I call after him. He doesn't answer. I look back and try to discern what he could have possibly seen, but there is not a soul. There is just the trees and the desert grasses and nothing else.

My brother bursts out of the house, a shotgun in his hands. "Son of a bitch," he says again.

"Whoa," I say. "What are you doing?"

"I'm not sitting here on my ass while some creepshow wanders around my goddamn property!" he says. He reaches into the waist of his pants and pulls out a pistol—a Glock 17. He shoves it at me. "Here."

"What the hell?"

"Take this! You stay here and watch the house! Who the hell knows who these assholes are!"

"But Bear, I swear to God, I didn't see anyo—"

"Just take the goddamn thing, damn you!"

I reluctantly take the pistol. It hangs limply in my hand. I've no idea what to do with such a thing.

"I got my phone," he says. "I'll call if I see anything." Then he dashes out into the wilderness without another word. I watch him recede into the mesquite scrub.

I stand there on the patio, frozen, gripping the pistol. I cover the grill, conscious that these invisible watchers, if they exist, could use the light of the flame to see me. Then I go inside and turn off the lights in the house, and I return to the patio and I stand in the shadows in the corner, the pistol clutched in my fingers.

I cannot imagine who or what Bear saw out there, or why it could have irked him so. He has always been impetuous, but I have not ever thought him the sort to go running into the wilderness at night with a gun.

I stand there for what seems like hours, not moving, trying to breathe as little as possible so my breath makes no frost. I listen for steps, for the shifting of branches or sand, for the pop of a gun. But there is silence.

Then I hear it.

A faint moaning sound, low and agonized.

I freeze and cock my head, listening. It comes again, a long, miserable exhale, and it seems very close, and yet also oddly muffled.

I peer at the wilderness beyond the patio. I can see no movement. I feel my blood pumping in my hands.

The moan comes again, and I realize where it is coming from: not in front of me, but behind me. It is coming from inside the house.

For a moment I freeze, unsure what to do. Then I slowly turn around, peering into the windows. Though the light is low and weak, I can see the house is empty. And yet the moan comes again, this time louder yet still queerly muffled. It seems like it is coming from inside our living room, less than a dozen feet away from where I stand.

I search every shadow, my eyes wide. But I can see nothing in the house.

I creep to the glass sliding back door, stop, and look back at the mesquite trees. There is no sign of Bear. I consider calling him, but I don't wish to bring anyone's attention to him, wherever he is.

I place my hand on the handle of the back door, and I slowly slide the glass door open.

I stare into the living room. For a long time there is nothing. But then I hear the moan again.

It is a woman's voice and it is so close by, muffled like they are lying under a pile of blankets in the middle of the living room—but I can see no one there.

The room is empty. I am sure of it.

But the moan comes again, and this time there are words in it, miserable and low: "*Ayuda... Ayuda, por favor...*"

I go cold as a thought enters my head:

The sound is coming from underneath the living room carpet. Maybe underneath the house itself.

"*¿Hay alguien?*" asks the voice. Its words are indistinct, like she is speaking from the basement—but as far as I am aware, we have no basement. "*Por favor, ¿hay alguien ahí fuera?*"

I stare at the living room carpet, unsure what to say or do.

"*Por favor, si estás ahí fuera, déjame salir,*" says the woman's voice. "*Por favor. Por favor, por favor, déjame salir de aquí!*"

There is a bang, and the living room carpet pops up very slightly.

"Oh, my God," I say.

"*Por favor!*" cries the muffled voice. Another bang, and the carpet pops up in the very center of the room, like there's a trapdoor just below it. "*¡Estoy tan sediento! Necesito agua, y… Y mi bebé… Mi bebé, mi bebé! ¿Dónde está mi bebé?*"

I put down the gun and kneel and begin feeling about the carpet. "Hold on!" I shout. "Just…just hold on, I'll get you out!"

The banging grows louder, more frantic. The carpet twitches like the skin of a drum.

"*¿Dónde está mi bebé?*" screams the voice. "*¿A dónde llevaron a mi bebé?*"

I pull and wrench at the carpet, but it will not give. The voice is screaming now, sobbing and shrieking, and the carpet is dancing, jumping, leaping in the center of the room as she shouts, "*¡Mi bebé, mi bebé! ¡Tráemelo de vuelta a mí, bastardo!*"

I dash into the garage and root around in our tools and pull out an Xacto knife. I run back into the living room and the voice is screaming now and I fall to all fours and I slash at it, wrenching it up and ripping the blade through it, trying to penetrate it, trying to stuff my fingers through so I can tear it away and let her out, let this girl out, let her free.

A growl as the carpet gives way. Below it is the carpet pad, ancient and yellow and filthy, and I claw at it and rip it away.

But below the carpet pad is bare concrete.

There is no trapdoor. There is nothing.

"What?" I say aloud.

The room is silent. The voice is gone.

I kneel on the ruined carpet in the faint moonlight, staring at the blank concrete. The knuckles of my left hand are bleeding from where the knife nicked me.

"Hello?" I say. "*¿Estás ahí?*"

But there is nothing.

Then Bear charges through the open back door, and he stands there, panting and breathing hard, shotgun still clutched in his hands. He does a doubletake and stares. "What the hell is going on?"

I look back down at the concrete under my knees.

"YOU'VE GONE NUTS," FUMES BEAR as we walk down the hill to the motel in the night.

"I heard it," I say. "I did. It was real."

"Hearing women in the goddamn floor? You've gone nuts."

"I haven't. I swear, I swear to God, Bear, it happened."

"Yeah, yeah, yeah." Bear stops at the corner of the motel and peers around the corner. "I saw him go this way. I know I did."

"You think I'm the crazy one, but you're the one chasing imaginary people with a gun."

"He wasn't imaginary! I saw him, goddamn it! I did! He's got to be out here somewhere!" We start off across the parking lot.

"What'd he look like?" I ask.

"I don't know. Like a guy. A man in white. Just come on."

We enter the U of the motel and walk from one arm of rooms to the other, looking for any sign of anyone or their passage. Bear peers into the windows of each room, but there is no one. All the world is vast and dark and empty, it seems, except for I-20 in the distance, white and shining and full of cars.

"Shit," Bear says. He stands at the edge of the parking lot, peering at the highway. "I guess they're gone, whoever they were." He glares back at me. "I suppose we ought to get back up to the house and fix what you did to the damn carpet."

We walk back to the side road that leads up to the house. Then I stop and look over my shoulder.

"You see someone?" asks Bear.

I walk along the motel rooms, gazing in the darkened windows.

"Well, did you?" he asks.

"I don't know. Maybe."

Finally I come to the room next to the check-in office— the room with the hatch.

I look at the floor. The hatch is closed, the linoleum smooth and unbroken. It is exactly as we left it.

Yet as we walked across the lot just now I am sure I saw a gleam of metal there, like the steel door was open, raised from the floor.

I watch the linoleum. It does not move. But I cannot help but fight the feeling that someone is down there.

"*¿Estás ahí?*" I ask softly. "*¿Puedes escucharme?*"

But there is no answer.

"You see anything or not?" asks Bear.

I keep staring in through the window, but there is nothing.

I follow Bear back around the motel to the house on the hill.

WE DON'T DISCUSS ANY OF it the next day. Instead we go about removing the plumbing from the rooms in near silence, then begin the slow, back-breaking process of scraping up the linoleum on the floors, followed by the adhesive still stuck to the foundation.

We leave the room with the hatch alone. Possibly because we know that scraping up linoleum that's adhered to a trapdoor would be hard. Or perhaps something about the room simply unnerves us.

As evening falls my brother says, "When do you need to go back to Houston?"

"Was planning to go in the next day or so."

He stares into the brilliant red sunset, the sun little more than a smear of blood on the horizon. "I'm thinking we've earned a night off," he says. "There's a bar over in Thortonville I noticed on the way in."

"Yeah?"

"Yeah. Looked crowded. Want to give it a shot?"

"Sure."

We shower and put on some half-decent clothes, though we have few of these—my wardrobe was almost entirely purchased from Walmart, and much of it is ill-fitting. As night falls Bear drives and I sit in the passenger seat as his truck bumps and jumps on its way to the highway.

I keep looking out the window at the flats around the motel, the mesquite trees short and straggly. For some reason I cannot help but feel that we are being watched, that I will search through the thorny branches and the tiny streaks of leaves and spy a human form among them, watching us depart.

But there is nothing. We are alone.

THE BAR IN THORTONVILLE IS more of a grill and lounge. It is brightly lit—something that makes my brother scowl—but it has pool tables and cheap steak and beer in clean glasses. We devour two ten-ounce ribeyes and drink beer and watch other people play pool. We do not speak, for neither of us feels comfortable here. We are too used to the silence and the loneliness of the Oasis.

My brother mops up grease with a twist of bread and stuffs it into his mouth. "Only got a couple more weeks of work, I reckon."

"Think so?"

"Yeah. Then it's just all about shipping in shit at the right time and getting it all installed. Hanging drywall won't be anything new for us. Finish line's in sight."

I say nothing. I watch a group of men playing pool. Two of them look mutinous, like there's been some foul play.

"I think it's just the aloneness of it all," my brother says suddenly.

"Huh?"

"Being alone. Alone in that place. Just flat around you and nothing else. I think it drives you crazy, maybe, a little. Like someone who stares at the sun for too long. Or maybe..."

He trails off. He doesn't want to say it. I don't either.

"It's a goldmine," he says. "And there aren't a lot of goldmines anymore for people like us."

"What do you mean?"

"I mean shit's changed. Used to be you could go almost anywhere in America, find decent work, get a house, get a pension, get a family, and you wouldn't have to tear your hair out or go into debt or get arrested crossing the street. That's what all these fellas here are doing, flocking around the frack sites with their trailers. Who knows how long that will even last. But, like—look at me, little brother."

"I am."

He turns to me, his eyes suddenly bright. "No, I mean—
look at me. You know me. You know what I've done. What
I've come back from."

I look at him, and nod.

"I'm no angel," he says. "But I'm clean. But that don't
matter now. You see a man like me ever making a decent
life for himself these days? I mean, really?"

I say nothing. The honest truth of it is that, on paper
at least, I am a far more acceptable person than Bear is
these days, and I have immense trouble imagining myself
succeeding at anything anymore.

"That motel—that goddamn, stupid motel—that
might be my last shot at something," says Bear. He drains
his beer. "Or maybe I've already peaked. And all that's left
is the decli—"

He never finishes the sentence. Because then the bar
fight breaks out.

IT IS LIKE MOST BAR fights, in that it is loud, short, and stupid. Within less than a minute it is over, and there is blood
on the floor from where someone was stabbed, and the sheriff's deputies and the ambulance are there, and then the
entire crowd is in the parking lot and everyone is recounting
and re-enacting and reviewing the debacle like it was not
three drunk fools slapping at each other on a pool table but
was instead the assassination of some noble dignitary. The

deputies and the sheriff wearily take everyone's stories, and
names and numbers and all the rest of it, and Bear and I sit
on the curb and wait, yawning.

Finally the sheriff gets to us. He is a tall, older man with
a kind but patrician face that is broad and fleshy, especially
about the neck and ears. His pad and pencil look tiny in
his hands. He looks us over from behind his wire-framed
glasses, an expression that is neither surprised nor pleased.
"Names, please."

"Bear Pugh," says my brother.

He begins to write. "And where are you from, Mr. Pugh?"

"Over in Coahora."

"And your business there?"

"Fixing up a motel."

The pencil stops moving. He frowns at his pad, then
looks at Bear quite hard. "In Coahora?"

"Yes."

"What motel?"

"Huh?"

"I said—what motel?"

"Hasn't had a name in a while."

The sheriff continues watching Bear. "Is it the Moon
and Stars?" he asks.

Bear and I exchange a look.

"Yeah, it is," says Bear.

The sheriff looks at Bear, his eyes still narrowed. "How
do you spell your last name, Mr. Pugh?"

Bear spells it for him.

The sheriff thinks for a while. "And...are you related to Corbin Pugh?" he asks.

Bear and I look at one another again, surprised.

"Why?" asks Bear.

"What do you know about that motel, son?" asks the sheriff.

"What is there to know?"

The sheriff just watches him. It is clear he is a man accustomed to getting answers, not giving them.

"I know it's old and falling apart," says Bear. "I know I own it now."

"Do you."

"What's this all about? What's going on?"

The sheriff thinks again, his face screwed up as he takes in the size of the crowd. "Well," he says with a slight sigh. "This is a curious situation. If you'd really like to learn a little more, you might have to wait a bit. This will take me a while. There's a decent Allsup's just down the road where we could talk. If you come back there in the morning around eight, I should be there. I'd be curious to find out how you came to be here, Mr. Pugh. And how much you know."

THE NEXT MORNING BEAR AND I wait in the Allsup's parking lot, watching a stream of F-150s pull up and depart, and pull up and depart. Finally the sheriff's prowler arrives and he steps out, placing his flat-brimmed hat on his head as he does so.

Bear rolls down his window and waves, and the sheriff approaches. "I only have a minute," says the sheriff. "Let me grab a coffee first."

When the sheriff exits the gas station with a giant Styrofoam cup in his hands, Bear and I get out and wait for him.

"What happened with the fight?" I ask.

"Stitches and jail. Nothing unusual. You boys sleep well?"

"Well enough. What's this all about now?" asks Bear.

"I guess I should introduce myself," says the sheriff. "Sheriff John Corddry." We shake hands. His grip is intimidating.

"What's going on?" asks Bear.

"First," says Corddry, "I would like to know more, if possible, about what you plan to do with that motel."

"What most do with motels," says Bear. "Rent it out to people."

The sheriff says nothing. He just waits for more.

"There's a high demand for rooms," I offer.

"All right," he says. "Is that all?"

"What else would there be?" asks Bear.

"How did you come to be in possession of it?"

"I bought it from my cousin," says Bear, "who inherited it from Corbin when he died."

"And...what do you know about Corbin himself?"

"What do *you* know about Corbin?" asks Bear.

Corddry allows a small, humorless smile. "I asked first."

"I know he ran that motel during the oil crisis days," says Bear. "I know it was a hopping place."

"A hopping place. It was that. So—that's all you know?"

We shrug. "That's it," says Bear.

"We don't know that much about that side of our family," I say.

"Wasn't aware there was much to know," says Bear.

The sheriff looks around, like he's slightly worried he might be overheard. "Well. I suppose someone owes you the truth. You're bound to hear it eventually, so it might as well be from someone reasonable." His words are careful, deliberate. "I'll say I'm a bit of a rarity in these parts these days, because I've lived in Coahora all my life. I was here back when that motel was in its peak days. I didn't know Corbin Pugh personally, of course, since I was just a kid. And, of course, I was raised in the church. Back when we used to all be God-fearing folk around here."

"What's that got to do with it?" asks Bear.

"I'm getting to that. These parts are full of small towns, and small towns talk, and gossip. And back then, it was known… Well. How should I put this." Again, the small, humorless smile. "I would say, son, that back then if you had a little money in your pocket, and you wanted to get your pecker sucked, there was always a girl in a room at the Moon and Stars."

There is a long silence.

"Huh?" says Bear.

"It's not like it was a big secret or anything," says Corddry. "You get used to it, working in law. Every good, upstanding town has a place where folks can put a toe out of line." There's a plumminess to his tone, a boys-will-be-boys sort of resignation.

"You're... You're saying our motel was, like...a whore-house?" asks Bear.

"I don't know if I'd put it *that* way," says Corddry. "But it was known that if you wanted a quick pump, or to pop your cherry, that was where you'd go. And Corbin Pugh could make it happen for you."

Bear stands there for a moment without saying anything. "So we bought a small-town brothel without knowing it," he says.

Corddry looks at us, his face strangely closed. I can tell right away that there is something more he knows, something he's keeping from us, but I can tell not to ask. "I'm sure it won't hurt your business much," he says. "These boys from Pennsylvania or South Dakota won't know or care. But I figured you'd want to know—and I wanted to know what your plans were."

"Plans?" I say.

"We got enough on our hands with all the new people in town," says Corddry. "You can see why just from tonight. But two Pugh boys buying the Moon and Stars..."

"There's plenty of money to be made legally," I say. "We don't need to do anything illegal."

Corddry's gaze rests on Bear for a moment, and I know he can see Bear's history there. A cop can smell a junkie a mile away, former or otherwise. Then his eyes dance over me, and hover briefly on my left hand, and the wedding band there. He seems to take heart in the sight of it. "Well. That's good to hear." He gives us two of his cards. "If you boys ever need anything or have any questions, you let me know—all right?"

I tell him we will. Bear remains silent and still.

"Good morning to you," he says. He tips his hat, climbs back into his prowler, and drives away.

AFTERWARD WE SIT IN BEAR'S truck, not moving or speaking.

"You think he's right?" he says finally. "That... That Corbin was some kind of a pimp?"

"Yes," I say.

"Christ. Christ almighty."

"But I think he's wrong about it, too," I say.

"What do you mean?"

"He makes it sound like it was small. Just one or two girls in the rooms or something."

"And?"

"You remember those photos we found? The Polaroids of the girls looking in through the transaction window?"

"Yeah?"

"Those photos—I think he was cataloguing which ones were his girls. I think they were all working for him. Which ones he got to take a cut from. And there had to have been at least fifty of those photos."

Bear looks out the window. "Shit..."

I say nothing, thinking of those faces in the pictures—all those girls, some barely older than twenty. I think about what they did in those rooms, what was asked of them.

"It was forty years ago," says Bear.

"Yeah."

"And Corbin's dead. This has got shit all to do with us. We already gutted the damn place."

"Yeah."

"Fuck this," says Bear. He starts his truck and puts it in gear. "Fuck it."

He pulls out and we start off down the highway, back to the motel.

"You said Dad worked there," I say quietly.

"Huh?"

"You said Dad worked at the motel. Back when he was a kid."

Bear drives along in silence.

"I wonder what he did," I say.

WE PULL BACK IN CLOSE to mid-morning. When we drive through the motel parking lot I feel Bear slow a little, and I know he's doing the same that I am, looking from room to room and imagining what happened there.

"Jesus," says Bear. "What the hell kind of a guy comes here to get laid."

"Huh?"

"You saw what the rooms looked like before," says Bear. "God. Can you imagine buying a fuck in a room like that?" He laughs suddenly, a nasty, angry sound. "Goddamn. How sad do you have to be to make that happen?"

"It doesn't bother you?"

"Bother me? No. Why would it? We ripped out everything in that place. Anything that touched a bit of whoring is long gone, hauled off in that dumpster. I mean—are you shocked?"

"Shocked?"

"Shocked to find out that a relative of our father was a goddamn scumbag?"

I say nothing.

"Dad and all the people like him," says Bear. "I'm tired of them hanging over my shoulder. These goddamn rough-necks pulling down one, two, three hundred grand a year. We deserve a piece of that." He guns the engine and we head for the house. Then we go down to the motel and we do our day's work, and we go to bed without another word.

I HAVE FEW MEMORIES OF my father.

He left when I was very small, and there was a lot going on besides. In the aftermath of it all we barely even had any photographs of him. Even his image, his likeness, is little more than a ghost to me now.

But the one memory I retain of my father that is quite clear is him pacing in our kitchen, back and forth and back and forth, rubbing the back of his head and clenching his fists and pinching his chest, pinching it hard enough to leave bruises (I would see the bruises later, I recall, the spots of black blooming across his bare torso), and he is cursing over and over again, hissing: "Fuck! Fuck! Fuck! Fuck this. Fuck this. Fuck them! Fuck this. Fuck this."

I remember that we would respond to these fits as if they were tornadoes, me and my mother and Bear fleeing into the bedrooms or closets and trying not to mention what was building outside. And we would not go out. It was too dangerous.

For all my life, I never wondered how my father came to be such a person. I had always just thought it was something stuck inside him, like a shard of stone wedged up against a bone in him.

But now, as I fall asleep, I wonder.

I AM NOT SURE WHEN I hear it. It is a sound I am accustomed to, a sound I long to hear and yet recoil from—the sound of a child crying in the night.

"Alice?" I mutter. "She's awake." My elbow jerks out, seeking to rouse my wife from slumber—but she is not there.

I open my eyes. I see the ceiling of the house. I remember where I am, far from my family—and yet I still hear the child crying.

I slowly sit up, listening hard. The crying does not fade. It goes on and on, reedy in the night, very distinct and very real.

"Bear?" I call out. "Do you hear that?"

There is no answer. I wriggle out of my sleeping bag and go to his room and turn the light on.

His sleeping bag sits empty on the floor. I see no sign of him anywhere.

"Bear?" I call again, louder.

Still there is no answer. Just the sound of the infant child wailing. I slowly begin to realize it is coming from outside—out back.

I walk down the hallway to the living room, where the slashed carpet awaits me. I look out the patio windows and see the mesquite trees, silvery and shimmering in the moonlight.

I can still hear the crying child. I am sure the sound is coming from out there, in the trees somewhere.

"Bear?" I whisper. "Bear, where are you?"

No answer. Just the infant, shrieking somewhere in the wilderness.

Then I see him.

He walks through the clearing in the mesquite trees in a slow, lumbering gait, a tall male figure in white. There is something almost processional to his movements, like he is following some sacred parade, attending to a holy rite amidst the moonlit trees.

I see he has something in his arms—a bundle, wrapped in white cloth. It is twitching and writhing, and then the sound of the cries peaks, and I see a tiny, angry fist emerge from the bundle of white cloth.

It is a baby. The thing in white is carrying a baby.

"Oh, my God," I whisper.

I watch as he fades into the mesquite trees, and is gone. And yet the crying of the child continues.

I am shaking all over and my blood is buzzing but I cannot just stand there, I cannot just sit and listen as this thing in white carries the child into the wilderness. I throw open the patio doors and stumble out into the wilderness beyond, running through the mesquite trees, dodging their branches and thorns, listening for the sound of the crying baby, running this way and that.

What I will do when I find it, I don't know. But I must do something.

I pause, cock my head, listen, and run on. It is always so close, and yet always receding, always drifting away.

And then the crying stops. Abruptly.

I freeze, my breath misting in the night air. I strain to listen, but all I can hear is the sound of the wind in the trees.

I walk on into the trees, peering through them, looking for any sign of the thing in white and the crying child. But I have lost them. They are gone.

Then I hear the footsteps. They are large and loud, like a giant walking through the brush. I crouch low and wheel about, looking for their origin, and then I see him.

It is the man in white, walking through a clearing some fifty feet from me. He is so tall, over six and a half feet, and his face is wreathed with shadow. He is not carrying the bundled child anymore. Now he carries a ball-peen hammer in one hand, and his hands and shirt front are splashed with bright red blood.

I stare at him, overcome with horror. Though I am sure I make no noise, the man in white stops.

And then, as if feeling my gaze, he slowly turns to look right at me.

The next thing I know I am running, sprinting through the trees, indifferent to their thorns or clawing branches. I am too frightened to scream, to think, to speak, to look behind me to see if he is following. I just run until I get back to the house, and I see that the lights are on and someone is standing in the living room, looking out at me.

It's Bear. He sees me and his mouth opens in surprise, but I don't stop moving, I run to the far side of the living room, my back pressed to the wall, looking out at the mesquite trees past the patio.

"Christ almighty," says Bear. "Where have you been?"

I try to talk but I realize the sounds I am making aren't anything close to human speech, they're just strangled half-screams. He kneels beside me and places one hand on my shoulder, and suddenly it's like we're children again, my brother seeking to understand what was done to me.

"What happened?" he asks. "What's out there?"

"He killed a child," I say. "He was walking with a baby out there and I think he... I think he killed the baby."

"Wait. What? A baby? Who?"

"A man in white. Maybe the one you saw. I couldn't see his face."

Bear studies me for a moment. Then he goes to his room and gets the shotgun back out. "I'll go look," he says.

"No. No, don't. Something's not right here. Something's wrong with this place, Bear. I don't think we're alone here."

"What do you mean?"

"I don't know what I mean. I just feel like there's someone out there, in the trees. Or in the rooms, when we're not looking. But when I look, they're gone."

He says nothing, not moving.

"Don't you feel it?" I ask. "Can't you tell that something's wrong here?"

"I think something's wrong with your head," he says. "There's been something wrong with you since you got here. I think maybe you had a nervous breakdown in Houston and now that you have to go back you're having another."

"You said you saw a man in white in the trees."

"Yeah. I saw a guy. Not a man carrying a baby around, or killing it out there in the back. My God, little brother. Do you hear what you're saying? Don't you know what you sound like?"

I bow my head, still too shaken to even truly process his words. But then I remember.

"Where did you go, Bear?" I ask.

"Huh?"

"I came to look for you before I went outside. But you were gone. Where did you go?"

"I went down to the motel. Just to look around."

"Just to look around?"

"Yeah. I got cagey. Went to go make sure nothing was wrong."

"And you didn't hear me?"

"No. No, I did not."

He does not meet my eyes. He has that shifty look that is all too familiar to me.

"Let me go look," says Bear. "I got cagey, and maybe I was right to get cagey. You stay here and keep an eye on the house."

He leaves. I do not protest.

I sit there for a moment in the living room, suddenly feeling sure that the man in white will peer in through one open window at me. But he does not come.

My mind turns to Bear, how he would not meet my eyes, how he seemed so anxious.

An idea calcifies in my mind, a very strange one.

I stand and slip out the front door of the house and walk down the hill to the motel, always peering about me in the dark, listening for the crush of brush as someone follows— but there is no one.

I go to the room with the hatch door. The panel of lino-leum flooring is shut, and the electrical socket that hides its handle is in place—but the screw is missing.

I pry the plate away with a fingernail, grasp the handle, and pull the flooring up.

The hatch is closed. But there is a smudge of grease on the face of the combination lock, and the combination code now reads 1839.

I try to turn the handle on the hatch, but it does not open. It is locked. Yet, oddly enough, I remember what the combination was when we first found the hatch—1946.

I begin to shut the linoleum flooring, but suddenly I catch a whiff of something—stale cigarette smoke and bad whisky and sweat, a masculine musk.

I stand there for a moment, smelling the odor, fruitlessly seeking its source. Then I return to the house.

Bear arrives soon after me. "Nothing. See anything here?"

I shake my head.

"Well. Shit. Maybe we just ought to go to bed, then. Put this whole night behind us."

I agree. I return to bed, but I do not sleep. And I close the door, perhaps in case someone walks down the hall and peers inside.

IN THE MORNING I PACK what few belongings I've accrued here and load up the truck to return to Houston to take care of my affairs.

"Are you going to be all right?" my brother asks.

"I guess." I look at him hard. "Are you?"

"I'm pretty good at doing shit all, so yeah."

I hold his gaze for a moment. The telltale shiftiness is gone, but something else has changed. It's hard to tell what. He has combed his hair, I realize, and shaved a little, and his shirt is clean. It's been a long time since I've seen Bear like this.

I suddenly think perhaps he actually is going to be okay. Something about him is different. More focused, more confident.

We embrace. Then I get in the truck and go.

I MEET ALICE AT A Bill Miller outside of the Woodlands and we sit over plates of cooling brisket and beans and make fumbling attempts at speech while construction workers come and go for their takeout.

She is as I remember her. Pale and thin with large, watchful eyes and an unflinching gaze. A seeming frailty that hides the hardness in her thoughts. Even now I can see the steel in her soul and I remember why it is that I loved her and married her in the first place.

And yet, we are silent. She does not bring up our daughter. We do not embrace. We do not touch. You would not think us husband and wife, to look at us. You would never imagine that together we had brought life into this world.

"I'd say you look good," she says finally.

I nod, waiting for more.

"But you really don't," she says.

"I've got a job. All that matters."

"Is it?"

I say nothing.

She sighs. "I don't know how to do this," she says.

"Me neither."

"No, I mean—I don't know what the steps are, what steps to take, because I don't know where we are. I barely even know what's going on."

"What do you mean? Going on with what?"

"Are you gone? Are you really gone?"

"You were the one who left. You should know."

"Sometimes it is impossible to talk to you." She sighs and sits back. "Even this, even leaving you, you leave up to me. It's up to me to figure out what we need to do. The car. Closing up the apartment lease, since you just walked out on it. Insurance. Loans. All that, I have to figure out."

"We don't have much left on our loans."

"God, how the hell would you know? When's the last time you looked?" She stares at me hard. "Am I taking you off Kendra's pick-up list?"

"Her what?"

"Jesus. For school. I can take you off it, you know. So you can't snatch her up. Do I need to do that? Be straight with me here."

"Christ. You think I'd take her?"

"Well, I just don't goddamn know anymore. I don't know where you've gone."

"I told you. I'm in Coahora."

"That's not what I mean. I mean here." She taps the side of her head. "You were gone long before I left, or before you went out there. You just went somewhere angry, and I could never figure out why and I could never bring you back. You were healthy. Kendra was healthy. We didn't have a lot of money, but we had enough. Wasn't that enough?"

I say nothing.

"You've got to talk to me," she says. "You've got to say something. I can't help us get through this and I damned sure can't help you if you don't talk. I know there's not, like, a big white space there behind your eyes."

"I'm not stupid."

"That's not what I'm saying."

"I might not have been a bigshot but I brought in steady paychecks for you and her."

"God. That's not what I'm talking about. This isn't about your ego. Can't you hear that?"

We stew in silence for a moment. I eat a mouthful of beans and do not look at her.

"I'm going to write down a list of things for you to sign," she says, sighing. "I'll do the paperwork, you just need to sign it. I'll even put the little tabs on it so you know where. And I'll need a mailing address, I guess, to send it to you. How many days do you have in town?"

I shrug.

"Least you could do is help my dad move all the stuff out of the apartment. He says he can do it himself but he's got that shoulder thing again. Do you have a place to stay the night?"

"I can sleep in the truck."

"Shit. What is the matter with you? Did you forget how to be civilized? You can sleep on my parents' couch. I know Kendra would be happy to see you."

I say nothing.

"You haven't asked about her," she says.

I blink and try to think of the words.

"I thought if there was something to say," I say, "you would have said it."

"God. Enough. Come on."

IN THE SHADOWS OF MEN

I HELP HER FATHER MOVE our belongings while Alice supervises. It is all done in a frosty, unbearable silence, a silence so heavy it hurts my bones. I used to belong to these people, and they to me, but now no longer.

I do not eat with them at evening. Instead I go to a chicken place and eat in my truck in the flat blue light of a parking lot lamp by some nameless tangle of interstates that seem to be everywhere in Houston. The lot is enormous and empty, a yawning gulf of asphalt and faded paint. Housed in the bland strip mall beyond is a seedy honkytonk and some kind of furniture store.

I watch the people leaving the honkytonk, and suddenly I am overcome with a desire to go in. Suddenly there is nothing I want more than to go in and drink a beer and smell cigarette smoke and find a woman or a girl in the red-blue light and take her...somewhere. Anywhere. Here in the truck if I need, my fingers gripping her soft brown flesh, my fingers invading the waist of her pants, prowling through her thatch of pubic hair as her breath whistles in my ear...

I hear a truck honk in the distance, and I feel moist wind on my face.

I stop and awake from my reverie. I realize I have left my truck and am halfway across the giant parking lot.

I look back at my truck, bewildered. I have no memory of getting out. Yet there are spilled fries on the ground beside the driver's door.

I return to the truck, shaking, get in, and drive to my in-laws' house.

***

WHEN I ENTER THE HOUSE I am presented with my baby girl like we are conducting an illicit deal and they are showing me a briefcase full of money. Alice's parents look on, tense and wary, willing to step in. Alice kneels beside the car seat bucket and unbuckles her carefully and extracts her and turns her around.

How changed she is, how changed. How she holds her head up, how fat her thighs are, her scalp is dark with growing hair, and her eyes are so bright, so full of personality. She looks at me, her head wobbling, and she crinkles her nose and makes that funny little face where she is so delighted she almost looks angry.

"She wants you," says Alice. There is a tone of joy missing from her voice now, and to hear it pains me.

I reach out and take my child.

"Hey, little girl," I say. "Hey."

My hands around her tiny ribs. The way her fingers explore my shoulders, my shirt, then my face. The smoothness of her cheeks, and the smell of her neck and ears.

Something inside me trembles. Just to know that this is mine, that I am responsible for this thing. And to know what a gap there is, between who I am and who I must be to live the life she needs me to live.

I have no roadmap showing me how to get to that place for her. There is this fuzzy picture in my head, of a father, of a husband, and I do not know who that man is but I know he is not me, and I think how strange it is to be haunted by this idea of a man who has never existed.

"How is she sleeping?" I ask hoarsely.

"Good," says Alice. "Good. She's sleeping good."

"Good," I say, giving her back. "That's good."

THAT NIGHT I SLEEP ON the old plaid sofa and stare at the popcorn ceiling and listen to the nocturnal movements of my wife and my child, the soft grunts and the keening cries and the weary shushing. How curious it is to hear it now, to trespass now upon the care given to my only child, care I once participated in.

Then I think of the thing I saw at the motel, the man in white holding the crying baby, and his hands wet and gleaming with blood as he gripped the ball-peen hammer. Suddenly that night is so present, too present, and the smell of mesquite is all over me and my skin is prickling from their many thorns, and I remember that Bear is alone there. I have left him alone in that place.

I get my cell phone and go to the kitchen and call Bear, just to hear his voice, to see if he is okay. He answers after four or five rings—or at least I think he answers, because I hear a slow, heavy breathing on the other end of the line.

"Bear?" I ask.

Then I hear other sounds, sounds I did not expect. There is a country song playing in the background, terribly loud. It is *Strangers*, by Merle Haggard, and there is the sound of many voices, all male, all laughing, like they're having a raucous, wild time, like a poker game.

"Bear?"

The heavy breathing continues, as does Merle Haggard's crooning, and the cackling of the men.

"Bear?" I ask again. "Is that you? Where are you?"

The breathing quickens, and something about it makes me think it is not Bear. It is too deep, too mushmouthed, too...strange. I somehow get the idea that my call is an intrusion to this person, and the sound of my voice angers him.

Then the call ends. Whoever it was has hung up on me.

I stare at the phone for a while, bewildered. I call Bear fifteen more times, but this time the calls never go through, and that night I do not sleep.

I SPEND ANOTHER DAY IN Houston, helping clear up my affairs. I try to call Bear repeatedly, but none of the calls go through. Then on a cool morning I load up my truck again and kiss my daughter on the head and I get back in the truck and I pull away.

I watch them in my jittering rearview mirror as I leave. My wife, standing on the sidewalk, and my daughter, situated on her hip. I am suddenly unsure what was it about domesticity that frustrated me so. Why did this chafe? Why did this make my insides burn? And why did I leave?

I pass the Fort Bend county limit. I stop at a Buc-ee's and park at the corner of the lot for gas and once I'm done I get back in and then I start crying. Big, ugly, awful sobs that I did not know I had inside me. I bite my knuckle and dwell on the pain to make it drive that sudden sadness out of me, and then I dry my eyes and get back on the road and I drive and I drive and I drive.

I ARRIVE IN THE EVENING and find both the motel and the house empty. I can see that Bear has done some work on the motel—he's stripped out a few of the old windows—but other than that, there is no sign of him. I try calling him on his cell, but again, the calls do not go through.

In the house, though, I find some sign of him, or a sign of someone, at least. First there is a smell of menthol cigarettes. Then I find a half-drunk six-pack of Miller Lite on the kitchen table, and beside that a stone ashtray. A few cigarette butts are piled at the edges of the ashtray, and almost all of them have a faint pink lipstick hue on the end.

I study this for some time, thinking. Then I go to Bear's room and see his sleeping bag has been replaced by a cheap twin bed with a single raggedy mattress, and it smells most decidedly of sex.

My phone rings. I see it's Bear, and answer it. My phone erupts with noise, and it's clear he's at a bar or club. "Hey!" he bellows. "Hey—you there?"

"Bear?" I say. "Can you hear me now?"

"Shit, my phone just blew up with missed calls from you. I take it you're back in town?"

"Yeah. Bear, where have you been? I've been trying to call you for days."

"What?" he shouts. "What do you mean for days?"

"I mean I've been calling you for days."

A pause.

"What?" he shouts.

"I don't know how to make this any simpler for you."

"Hey—hey, I'm at a place."

"Well, I goddamned figured. Most people are."

"It's in Odessa. It's a cool place. You ought to come out. I bet you need it after that trip."

"I bet I don't."

"You got to have some steam you need to blow off. Only makes sense." He gives me the address. "We'll be here an hour or two longer, just about."

"We?" I say, but he's already hung up.

IN THE SHADOWS OF MEN

I MEET BEAR AT A bar called Knott's, a seedy place with red and blue lighting and sticky floors and bathrooms that reek of urine from ten feet away. Despite this it is a thriving place, full of roughnecks and other men drawn to work the patch. I recognize it as a bad combination almost immediately. Money and frustration and machismo do not go well together.

I find Bear in a corner booth with a woman of about forty. She is very tan and wears a denim halter-top, and her hair and makeup are, to me, very Dallas Fort-Worth: big, blonde, and bold. Her lipstick is ruby red, and I notice a heart tattoo on her left breast, just below the collarbone.

"This is Shauna," Bear says as I sit down. "Say hello, y'all."

Shauna and I exchange greetings. "Nice to meet you," she says. I can tell she is not drunk, but close to it.

"How'd it go in Houston?" Bear asks.

I shrug, shake my head, and say no more.

"Figures," says Bear. "Goddamn."

"What's in Houston?" asks Shauna.

"Problems," says Bear.

We discuss the motel, the progress, the work. The windows. The flooring. The plumbing. Shauna seems bored. I can't blame her.

I notice Bear seems very animated, and I instinctively check his arms for any needle-marks, and squint through the gloom to see the state of his teeth. They suggest he is

65

clean, but he just seems changed to me. He's shaved and combed his hair again and even put something in it, and it swoops back away from his forehead—a queerly retro look I've never seen him affect.

When Shauna goes to the bathroom, I turn to him and say, "So—what's going on with you?"

"What do you mean?"

"I mean, a bar, a girl. I thought we were focusing on the work until the work was done."

"I am working. I'm also relaxing. We've worked our asses off."

I peer at him.

"What?" he says testily.

"You just seem different."

His face curdles. "Goddamn it," he says. "Goddamn it, I'm clean and you know I'm clean."

"I have a right to worry."

"You don't have a right to shit," he says. "I gave you this job, your bed, the work. And I'm giving you your cut. You don't have a right to tell me how to be on top of all that." He tosses back the rest of his beer resentfully. "I'm paying out."

We wait at the bar for Shauna. The screens above the bar depict a number of things: baseball, soccer, some streaming service designed for bars that appears to feature nothing but people attempting stunts and grievously injuring themselves; but two TVs show the local news. There is a report of a girl who's been missing for the past two days, and we watch as it cuts to the girl's parents, the father short and thick with a mustache and glasses as thick as a dictionary, the mother with spiky blond hair. They weep in the bright lights of the TV cameras, though we can't hear what they're saying. The report then shows a picture of a smiling girl of about twenty, with blond hair, tan skin, a silky blue and white polka-dotted shirt, and bright pink lipstick. The chryon at the bottom says, "LAST SEEN WEARING." Below that is the number to call if seen.

"Towns like this used to be small," says Bear. "Now it's big as hell, with big crimes."

"Hope the money's worth it," I say.

"It is," he says.

OVER THE NEXT FEW DAYS Shauna becomes a fixture at the Oasis. It's not clear to me where she actually lives—we do not talk much—but I suspect she is still living with her ex-boyfriend, who lives on one of the man-camps somewhere, possibly. It is all too vague and shifting for me to keep up with.

Our living conditions come to feel distressingly adolescent. The sounds of sex filter through the walls each night, and in the between-times—when I am in the kitchen or the living room, or anywhere at all, really—it seems like I am always encroaching on some intimate moment, like I should be somewhere else.

I try and broach the strange call I had with Bear in Houston, but he claims complete ignorance. "I don't know shit about Merle Haggard," he says. "I'm surprised you recognized the song. And I don't have that many friends."

"Then someone had your phone?" I ask.

"No way. Must have been, I don't know, a crossed-over call or something."

"It was weird," I say. "It was threatening."

"How can breathing be threatening?"

"It just was. I thought we had service out here. I had great service just a bit ago."

"We either got it or we don't. No in between. I don't know what to tell you."

"You boys got a broom around here?" asks Shauna, walking barefoot out of the hallway. She is wearing shorts and a large T-shirt—sleep clothes. She either just slept here or intends to soon.

"All the cleaning stuff's down at the motel, babe," says Bear.

"You could stand to work on this place too, you know," says Shauna.

"Then get a broom and hop to it."

Shauna rolls her eyes and opens the hall closet and begins rooting around. Her arrival kills our conversation, and for a moment we just sit there, half-heartedly drinking our beers.

"I think we can open before winter," says Bear confidently.

"Huh? Really? I thought we were shooting for spring."

"Nah. We're making good progress. We'd have to fuck something up big time to wait for spring."

This puzzles me. I know we are in no way close to being ready to open the motel in spring.

"I think we can do it before winter," says Bear, "because we'll have one less room to bother with."

"Huh?"

"I think you're right. I think we should close off the room with the hatch. It's weird. It's probably a liability thing. I've looked at insurance options, and fuck, I don't want to start that kind of a conversation. So we'll just close it up." He cracks open another Miller Lite and slurps at it but there's something strangely closed to his face.

"Have you done any work on that room?" I ask him.

"Huh? No. I've left it alone. Focused on the others. Not going to bother with it if we're not going to lend it out."

There's an awkward beat.

"Listen," Bear says. "Don't fuck with the hatch. Okay?"

"Huh?"

"Don't go down there. Don't go in that room. I don't anymore. I locked it up. Let's just forget about it. All right?"

I look at him. I can tell, somehow, that this is not a request.

"Okay," I say. "Sure."

"Found one," says Shauna. She hauls an ancient broom out of the hall closet. "God. I hope it stays together long enough to sweep all that hair off the bathroom floor. I swear, you boys…"

Bear leans forward to peer at the hall as she leaves. "Hey! At least pick up all the shit you hauled out before you go!"

"I'm not done yet!" she calls back as she goes into the bedroom.

"Hell," mutters Bear.

I stand up to go to my room. But as I pass the hall closet and all the random detritus Shauna has pulled out and left scattered on the floor, I pause.

Most of the objects are quite old. Pearl-snap shirts and cigarette lighters and an old boot polishing kit. Yellowed books on horses and the battle of San Jacinto. VHS tapes of the show *Rawhide* and lots of John Wayne movies. An ancient crackling football.

But one is familiar: a ball-peen hammer.

I stare at the hammer, lying on its side on the linoleum floor. The varnish is gone from its handle, so its wood is gray and splintering, and its head is black and rusting at the edges. It is altogether mundane, yet the sight of it makes me feel like my belly is full of ice.

"What?" says Bear.

I slowly kneel and pick up the hammer, holding it in my hands. I turn it over, and find that the wood near the head is discolored and dark.

"What is it?" says Bear.

I say nothing. I just take the hammer, go to my room, and sit on the floor and stare at it, thinking.

Was it real? Was what I saw out in the scrub truly real?

Do I catch the echoes of things that happened before in this place? Or am I going mad out here, or did I go mad a long time ago?

***

WE GO BACK TO WORK on the motel for the next three days.

Bear seems to do less and less work. He wakes up later, finishes earlier, spends more time with Shauna, spends time down in the city. He makes up many patently false claims about what he's doing—running errands, talking to insurance people, drumming up business—and he buys great deals of water and food and chips, which he brings to his room, and then I do not see them again.

He does not seem to care about whether I believe his story about his errands or not. Things do not matter anymore, not in this between-place. I know this now, as I sleep in my room. This place is like the rest of these flats. It is simply a place to get lost in.

We live, we work, we sleep. And then one night I awake in my room to the sound of a woman crying.

I sit up in my sleeping bag, and I listen to it for a while. I wonder if it is Shauna, but somehow I know it's not. It's not coming from Bear's room—I know what noises coming from Bear's room sound like now—but rather from outside, at the back of the house.

I get out and move through the hallways, all bluely lit and layered with shadows, all the corners whispering and a muttering rumbling through the floor, and I go to the sliding glass door in the back.

There is someone standing on the patio, gray-white in the light of the moon above. It is not the thing in white: it is a woman, short and thickly built with black hair. She is facing away from me, and though she is wearing a silk nightie, she is bruised and mussed and she has wounds around her wrists and ankles, like she has been bound up.

I stare at the back of her head as she looks out at the scrub beyond. Then I open the glass door and walk out to her.

She does not look at me. She keeps staring out at the trees. She is Latina, and young, and though her face is bruised and her lip is split I recognize her. I think I remember her from the Polaroid pictures we found in the check-in desk, so many days ago.

Without looking at me she raises her hand and points into the scrub, into the far corner of the yard. I have not studied what is out there—I have averted my eyes from this place since seeing the thing in white—but now that I look I think I see an old metal roof out there.

A shack, perhaps. Or a shed.

"*Mi bebé,*" says the woman.

I stare at her. I am breathing very hard now. My blood feels like it is going to break through my eardrums and flood down the sides of my head.

She turns to look at me, her dark eyes filled with tears. "*Mi bebé y yo.*"

I look into her face, uncomprehending. Then the branches in the scrub just behind her twitch, and something surges out, something tall and hulking and white, and it grabs her hair and rips her backward into the trees.

Her eyes never leave mine and her face never changes as she's pulled away. Then she is lost in the trees.

With a gasp, I awake in my sleeping bag.

I am in my room. I am alone. Perhaps.

I look around, bewildered and terrified. My eye falls on the closet door. The clothes within have shifted, and I can see the head of the hammer there, gleaming even in this low light.

THE NEXT DAY WHEN WE are finished with our labors I go back to my room, and I rummage in a bag in the corner until I finally pull out the card for Sheriff Corddry.

I think for a long while. Then I call and get his voice-mail, and I leave him a message asking if I could talk to him.

He returns my call the next day, when we're installing new flooring in the motel rooms. I walk away and answer, and after some pleasantries he asks, "What was it you'd like to talk about?"

"Corbin Pugh, specifically," I say.

"And what, specifically, would you like to discuss about Mr. Pugh?"

"I wanted to see if you knew anything about…about anything else he'd done. Like—beyond just the, you know. The prostitutes."

There's a long silence.

"You found anything out there, son?" asks the sheriff.

I look at Bear, who pauses in the middle of picking up a new roll of vinyl flooring. Bear looks up at me and studies me for a moment before going in one of the rooms.

"You there, son?" asks the sheriff.

"Yes, sir. I guess I'm just interested in learning more about him."

"In gossip, then." He sighs. "Well. If you want to come down to town, we can talk about it over lunch like civilized people. I've got a moment if you do."

I tell Bear I'm off. He doesn't seem surprised or bothered by it. Before I go, I grab the photo of Corbin and the woman—his wife, or so I've long assumed—and put it in my pocket.

I meet the sheriff in a diner, and we talk over plates of barbacoa and diced onion and refried beans. He watches me very closely from behind his square, modest bifocals. Accountant's glasses, almost. Were it not for his size and bearing, they would tempt you into thinking he was a placid man.

Sheriff Corddry maneuvers the meat and beans about on his plate with a workman's precision, arranging each bite before bringing it to his mouth. "What is it you've found up there that made you so curious about Mr. Pugh?" he asks carefully. He looks up at me, and I see the glint in his eye again: he knows more, but he's unsure whether or not to tell me. "It's a curious impulse—to hear something disreputable about one's family, and then go digging for more."

"My family never had much reputation to lose, to be frank, sir."

He wipes his mouth and nods. "I see. What is it you're looking to learn, exactly?"

"About the girls who worked for him. Who they were, and where they've gone."

"You want to track them down?"

"Is that possible?"

"I can't imagine how."

"None of them still live around here?"

"Not that I know of. And if they did work at the Moon and Stars, they sure aren't going to be forward about it."

"How many of them were there?"

He sits back from his plate, his face grim, and finally relents. "All right. There were about ten or so, at any given time. I don't know where they came from. Mexico, I'd assume. Some stayed on the property with him, I was told. Others were more transient."

"What happened to the girls when he was done with them?"

"What happens to that sort of girl, when they're done being that sort of girl? Maybe, if grace favored them, they found God and left that path. It all ended when the oil boom died in the eighties, either way." He fixes me in a hard look. "Are you trying to save them, son? To redeem them?"

"I don't know. Maybe I was trying to make up for what my uncle did."

He shakes his head. "Best to forget about it. People like that—they're made to be forgotten."

An image flashes in my mind: the girl on the porch, her eyes filled with sorrow, staring out into the mesquite.

"Why?" I ask.

I can feel the air grow colder between us. "It's been a couple decades, yes. But a lot of men went to the Moon and Stars. Men with land and oil. Many of them are still alive, and many of them still live around here. It'd be unwise to go dragging out childish sins. We have enough trouble managing the disruption that the Permian's brought. We don't need more."

I feel he is done talking about the girls, and I need to move the conversation. "What was Corbin Pugh like?"

"What was he like?" He allows a low laugh. "Goodness. You heard of a hooker with a heart of gold?"

I nod.

"Ever hear of a cuddly, sweet-tempered pimp?"

"No."

"Because there's no such thing. Corbin Pugh was a tough SOB, so to speak. I guess you have to be, to be in that line of work and deal with those sorts of women, and men. I heard stories as a kid that if you touched a girl without talking to Corbin first, he was liable to break your hand."

Another image flashes in my mind: the hammer, its wood dark and stained.

"Did he do anything to the girls?" I ask.

He looks at me as if I was an idiot. "When a girl gets into that line of work, she knows what she's getting into. Is there anything else you'd like to know?"

"Yes. Did he have a wife?"

For the first time, he seems surprised. "Corbin? A wife? No."

"No?"

"No. If so, I never heard of it."

I take out the picture of Corbin Pugh and the woman, and hand it to the sheriff. "That's him?"

The sheriff lifts his head and peers down his nose to make sure he's looking through the right part of his bifocals. "That's the man, if I recall. I never saw him that young, though." He cocks his head a little. "But the woman…"

"Do you know her?"

"No. I don't." He narrows his eyes at the picture. "Looks like she's wearing a ring. And maybe he is, too, but his arms are crossed."

"You think that could be his wife?"

"Maybe," says the sheriff. "But if she is, I've no idea what happened to her."

"So we don't know where Corbin's wife is," I say, "or where any of his girls are."

"What are you suggesting here, son?"

"I don't know. I just have pieces of a story and I'm trying to put it together."

He slowly sits back. "I was worried about you both, you know," he says. "You and your brother. Because to be honest, you seem like most people. You get to come here, make money, and go. But the rest of us, we've got to live here. We've got to live here with all the stuff everyone digs up. Now, I need to ask—do I need to worry about you?"

"I don't want to make you worry."

"Then why are you asking this? Why not just open your motel and make your money and go?"

"I don't know. I guess I have never understood the men in my family. And this is the closest I have ever gotten."

His gaze grows somewhat pitying. "The loss of church in the life of our people is a damaging thing," he says. "So many young men don't know themselves. They don't have any idea how to be decent men."

I say nothing. I cannot begin to imagine what church could help me with what I feel is following me. And I wonder what church the sheriff goes to, when he seems to feel so little concern for the girls who have passed through the Moon and Stars.

The sheriff glances up at the television. I follow his gaze. It's a report about the missing girl, the one I glimpsed at the bar with Bear and Shauna, the tanned young smiling girl with the pink lipstick and the blue and white polka-dotted shirt.

"They've been playing reports about her for a while," says the sheriff. "I feel a bit bad about it, you know."

"I can't blame you."

"No, no. I mean, I feel bad that I feel glad that it didn't happen here. So she's not mine." He looks at me balefully. "All these transients, these men that come and go. Missing persons cases are often impossible to solve. But that one will be doubly so."

He wipes his mouth, pays, and stands. Then he tips his hat to me, bids me good day, and returns to work.

I drive back up to the Oasis, my head full of poisonous thoughts. Of Corbin Pugh, and the many rooms at his motel, and the many women who might have been there— his wife, his girls—who have all vanished now.

I RETURN TO THE HOUSE to find an impromptu party is taking place. I hear it before I see it, hear the music—some quavering, husky-voice man—and I smell cigarette smoke, and I slink through the door, feeling every inch the younger sibling reluctant to bear witness to his brother's misdeeds so he won't have to lie to his parents.

Bear and Shauna, it seems, have brought back a friend—another tanned blonde named Mary Jo—and they greet me so loud when I walk through the hallway that I know they must be five beers deep apiece. Though Shauna and Mary Jo, it seems, prefer a kind of alcoholic seltzer I've never seen before.

"Figured it was time to cut loose," says Bear. "Enjoy ourselves. First time that's probably happened here in a while, huh?"

He goes out back to cook burgers on the grill, but by now it's clear that he and Mary Jo and Shauna are here to get drunk in a very big way.

I check my phone. It is three in the afternoon. I absently wonder what Shauna and her friend do for a living. I suppose it's this.

Mary Jo has, it seems, been talked into having sex with me. She indulges me, attempting to flirt with me, but all I can think of is the sound of an infant in the trees, and I wonder what my wife and child are doing right now back in Houston. I politely answer her questions, and parry her approaches, and courteously tolerate her presence. She grows more irritated with me as the afternoon goes on.

We eat. The burgers are rich and greasy and they fill the paper plates with cloudy brown fat. I watch Bear chewing, his eyes dull and dead beneath that odd retro haircut of his, and I know he is approaching stone drunk.

I go outside for air. I stare at the mesquite scrub and the skeins of clouds racing across the evening stars. For some reason the sight before me fills me with dread. I do not wish to be trapped in this old house with my brother, with the dark falling fast, closing us in, darkness hard and thick like a black wall spreading through the trees. I do not want to see what creeps in with it.

The door behind me opens. It's Mary Jo. "You come out here for a smoke?" she asks.

I shake my head.

"You got a smoke?"

I shake my head again.

"Hum." Her eyes glitter as they study me. "You look like your brother. But do you talk less, or listen more?"

I watch her for a moment. She looks back at me, flirty and interested and yet oddly defiant. Then out of nowhere I'm overcome with a queer impulse, a sudden, surging desire not to kiss her or touch her, but to take this woman and shove her backward up against the side of our house, one hand around her throat and the other ripping the front of her pants open, and then to look into her eyes as I penetrate her, to see the surprise and the fear and the submission there, and should her expression turn to joy then I'll turn her around and bend her over and take her from behind, to let her know how unimportant she herself is to this act, that her body and her person is no more than cotton in the field for me to harvest.

My blood burns hot. The night is distant. And somewhere there is the sound of crying.

I hear a rustling in the trees, and the moment breaks, and I look back at the mesquite.

And I wonder—do I see a figure out there, in white, looking back at me?

"What's wrong?" asks Mary Jo.

I look back at her, shaking. It was as if I'd been sleepwalking, just for a moment, but nearly sleepwalking through assault, through violence, through rape.

Just like back in Houston, when I awoke and found myself crossing the parking lot of the honkytonk.

And it is then that I wonder—are these impulses mine? Or do they come from somewhere else?

I slowly turn to look at Bear, sitting inside, beer clutched in his hand, scowling as he talks to Shauna, and I wonder if he is experiencing something similar.

I turn away from Mary Jo, and she makes a noise of indignant surprise, but she follows me and we sit down, me at the table, she beside Shauna on the couch. Shauna is smoking a cigarette, and Mary Jo resentfully bums one from her and lights it.

I watch the smoke unscrolling from their cigarettes. I smell it in the air, harsh and musky, and something stirs in my memory.

"I thought you all smoked menthols," I say suddenly.

"What?" says Shauna.

"It's nothing," I say. "I just thought you all smoked menthol cigarettes."

"I don't," says Shauna. "Those things are gross as hell."

The two women stare at me for a moment and exchange a glance. But Bear is watching me very closely, his eyes set far back in his skull.

I think of the house when I first came home from Houston. The pack of Miller Lites on the table—and the smell of menthol cigarettes in the air, and the butts in the ashtray, ringed with pink.

I look at Shauna and Mary Jo. Neither of them have pink lipstick—they are crimson and cherry red. I try to remember if I have ever seen Shauna wear pink lipstick, but my memories seem so distant and fuzzy now.

"After nothing for some damned long," says Mary Jo, "that's the first thing you say?"

I blink, and realize I had been lost in thought. "I'm sorry?" I say.

"You're weird," she says. She looks at Bear. "He's weird as hell."

Bear drunkenly nods his head. "It is true that he is a bit weird."

"Is he crazy? Or a faggot? Or what?"

He glares at her. "Don't call him that."

"Well, I'm just wondering," she says.

"Well don't. You don't know him. You don't know us. You don't know anything about any of this."

Mary Jo rolls her eyes. There's a long, awkward pause, broken only by the man on the speaker singing about how when you leave this world you leave it alone.

"You know what this place used to be?" asks Bear.

"A shithole?" says Mary Jo.

Shauna attempts to quiet Mary Jo, but she's not having it.

"No," says Bear. "It was a whorehouse."

That stops both women. They look at him, perturbed.

"What?" says Shauna.

"It was a whorehouse," says Bear. "Back in the seventies. The sheriff told us so. The guy who ran the place, he was like a pimp. We keep finding pieces of it. Photos of girls and the like. That's what this place used to be."

"That's horrible," says Shauna.

"It gets worse," says Bear. He stares off into the distance. "Because the guy who ran the place, the pimp—he was our grand-uncle."

"If you boys are going to try to resume the family business," says Mary Jo, "you're going to be the most incompetent pimps I ever known."

Bear smiles sardonically. "We didn't know when we bought the place. Just knew it belonged to a relation of ours.

But the hell of it was, our father supposedly worked here, when he was a kid. Can you believe that? He got stuck out here during the summers and he ran jobs for old Corbin Pugh. It's a hell of a thing to say, that our daddy worked at a damned whorehouse as a child." Bear cocks his head dreamily. "It makes you wonder, doesn't it? What he saw here. What he saw people do. What he learned. And how it changed him. How it changed him to think about men, and women. And I guess maybe that explains why he did what he did."

"Bear," I say.

But he is not stopping now. "I thought all fathers were just like him, you know," he says. "I thought it was just how men were. I thought every man would get drunk now and again and get so angry they took a hunting knife and stabbed holes in all the furniture. I thought it was normal, that a father would punch a toddler for wetting the bed. And that it was normal for a husband to beat the everliving shit out of his wife every once in a while, and put her in the hospital, for reasons even he couldn't explain."

There is a long, long silence.

"They pulled him out first," he said, nodding to me. "They left me there with them. I wasn't sure why. I guess maybe just because he was younger. People didn't think about that shit much in those days, or maybe Texas is just fucked up that way. But I was there for all of it. When he broke her head, and they put him in jail, I was the one who was with her for the hospital. All those tubes in her. All the beeping, the alarms, the nurses coming in to change bandages and drain this or that. And in the end, I was the only one with her when she died. And it was then that I realized none of this was normal. And I wonder now, here in this motel—is this where it started? Is this the place? Or was that always how that was gonna go?"

There is another long, awkward silence.

"I want to leave," says Mary Jo.

"Then leave," says Bear.

"I don't have a car," she says.

"And even if you did, you'd be too drunk to drive it," says Bear. He looks at me. "How deep are you?"

"Not very. I can drive you home," I say to Mary Jo.

"God. Fine." She stands and fixes Shauna in a hard stare.

"I'll go too," Shauna says reluctantly.

"That's fine," says Bear. "That's just fine."

The two women leave to go wait by my truck. I look down at Bear, slouching in the old recliner, beer clenched in his fist, a brooding look on his face, and suddenly I see all the ghosts of men I have never known that still haunt our lives.

"We should sell it," I say.

"Huh?"

"We should sell the motel."

"What?" He looks at me, a spark of disbelieving wrath in his eye. "What are you talking about?"

"This place. If you really think this is where all that started, we shouldn't be here. This place is poison, if that's so."

"We worked ourselves to the bone," he says. "*I* worked myself to the bone!"

"It'd be like drinking from a lead pipe, Bear. All that stuff staying with you, in your blood, all the time."

"We deserve this!" he shouts. He stands up. "We deserve this! Goddamn it, I am owed something from all this. I am owed success, I am owed a life. I am owed a place where I can take what's mine. I am owed that."

We look at one another for a long while. I suddenly feel uncomfortable leaving him here, alone with all these shadows, in this state. But then I hear Mary Jo impatiently shout for me, and he turns his back, and I walk away.

I DRIVE MARY JO TO her trailer park. It is, apparently, the same trailer park Shauna lives at. I stop in front of Mary Jo's trailer, and she gets out and walks in without a word. Shauna tarries behind.

"Is Bear all right?" she asks.

"No," I say.

"Are you?"

I don't answer.

"Has he had another party, since you've come back?" she asks.

"What? What party?"

"Those men who met at the motel, in the room. The only time he seemed happiest was the next day. But after that, he went weird."

I look at her, bewildered. She's drunk, but I can tell she's telling the truth, or she thinks she is. "What party? What are you talking about?"

"I don't know. I thought you knew. It was one of the first nights we met. It was almost like a dream. I spent the night at the house. And I woke up in the night and he was gone but I heard music coming from the motel. And I got up and went to the window and I could see a light in one of the motel rooms was on, but it was facing away from me. But I heard music coming from it, and a lot of men laughing."

"What do you mean?"

"What do you mean, what do I mean? I mean it seemed like Bear was having a party down there in the motel. I was sure he was. So I got my shoes on and I went out there and I got close to the corner and I remember seeing the light spilling out into the parking lot, and all the people moving across the light in the room, and the music playing really loud, and all the men laughing. Like they were having a great time."

"And then what?"

"And then I was thinking… I was thinking I ought to go around the corner and introduce myself. Walk in and ask for a drink. But for some reason…for some reason I didn't."

"Why?"

"Because I was scared. I was scared of the men in that room. I don't know why. I just… I just knew what was going on in that room was not for me. I wasn't supposed to be there. I wasn't supposed to see it. It wasn't for me, that's all I can say. Like I said, I almost thought it was a dream."

I stare at the sky in the horizon, queerly lit by the flare of the frack sites beyond. "This music," I say.

"Yeah?"

"Was it old? Old country? Or new?"

"Old. Pretty old."

I sit there for a long, long time without saying a word. "You shouldn't see Bear again," I say.

"What?"

"You shouldn't see him. Something's wrong with him. And wrong with that place, with the motel."

She stares at me. Then she quietly asks, "Do you see him too?"

"See who?"

"I don't know. But I feel like there's a man living on your property. Hiding in the corners. And I feel like I see him now and again."

I watch her a moment and then put the truck in reverse. "Don't go there again, Shauna. Don't call Bear and don't go there again, all right? Not until we're out of there."

"What are you going to do?" asks Shauna.

"I don't know. But don't go there again."

She gets out of the truck, and goes to her trailer. She looks back at me once before she goes inside, and I pull out and return to the highway and the darkness, and I wonder what I will find when I get to where I am going.

I RETURN TO THE MOTEL and I park at the edge of the parking lot but I go no further. I just watch the rooms, the windows, and the house on the very gentle slope above.

There is no movement. All the world is still except the clouds in the night sky.

I turn the truck off and I get out my big Mag-Lite and I walk across the parking lot to the room with the hatch. I hesitate before the window, but then I turn the light on and peer inside.

The room is empty. The panel of flooring is shut.

I check the doorknob. It is locked, as it is supposed to be.

I slowly rotate the beam and turn around, studying the other rooms. I am alone. I don't know why, but I was sure I would find Bear here.

I trudge my way up to the house, watching, listening. The trees and scrub are still and silent. The house is dark. I do not turn on the light as I walk inside.

I stand in the living room, listening. All is still. There is nothing.

"Bear?" I call.

There is no answer.

I go to the sliding glass door. I stare out at the land beyond. I remember the woman standing on the porch, pointing out at the corner, and the thing in white, stalking through the trees, its hands bloodied, its face lost in darkness.

No, I decide. No, I will not go there. Not if he is out there.

I stalk down the hallway, the beam of light shuddering on the carpet before me.

"Bear?" I say again. But once more there is no answer.

I come to his door and peer inside. His room is as it always is, messy and slovenly, the bed reeking of sex. But I shine the light inside and let its beam dance over the things scattered across the floor: the deodorant, the beer cans, the socks, the old shoes.

I walk inside. I am not sure what I am looking for, truthfully. Some sign, some scrap of something that could help me understand what is happening to my brother: who he is, where he has gone, what he has done.

Then my light lances across the carpet at the feet of an old dresser. I see indentations in the fibers, blocky corners pressed into the fabric, and I know that the dresser has been moved.

I walk to the side of the dresser and press my face up against the wall and shine my light in. There is something stuffed back there, perhaps haphazardly, perhaps drunkenly. It looks like a set of clothes.

I shove the dresser forward, reach behind, and pull the clothes out. As I jostle them the scent of menthol comes billowing out, old and faint but all too real. I have to pin my flashlight under my armpit so I can look at them in my hands.

A pair of jeans, with some kind of plastic jewels lining the back pockets. They are size zero. A young girl's jeans, I think.

As dread fills my mind I fumble in their crotch and I do not find any undergarments within. But the zipper is marred and tangled, as if it had been ripped open.

Yet it is the shirt that dismays me the most. It is silky, with blue and white polka dots. There is a faint brown splotch at the collar, and a patch of red beside it. It is ripped at the shoulder, like it was torn off of whoever had been wearing it.

I stare at the shirt in my hands. I turn it over, seeking other stains, other damages.

But I don't need to. For I know this shirt. I have seen it on the news in town, and in Odessa, and perhaps in countless other places as well.

The missing girl. The smiling young girl in all the pictures.

I think of the lipstick on the menthol cigarettes I found when I returned from Houston. It had been bright pink.

I think back to the news reports. Was her lipstick pink? Was that the color? I crouch there in the room, my heart pounding, trying to remember this while also desperately trying not to understand.

My mind spins more, faster and faster. About the water and chips and snacks Bear purchases that I never see again.

Almost as if he is feeding someone here. Keeping someone alive, someone hidden.

Then I hear the music.

I nearly scream at the sound of it. The sound of it is very faint, and it is not coming from inside the house. I know in an instant that it is from the motel. It is the only possible place.

I listen to it for a long while, frozen where I kneel in my brother's room. Then I stand and walk to my own room and peer through the window.

There is a light on in the motel below. And there is no doubt in my mind as to which room it is.

I cannot see into the room from this angle, but I can see the light spilling out into the parking lot, rich and golden. There are many shadows passing before it, like the room is full of people, moving back and forth.

A party. Like someone's throwing a party in that room.

My skin grows cold. I stare at the light for a long, long time. Then I walk down the hallway, breathing slow and deep, until I exit the carport and stand at the top of the hill, looking down at the motel.

I know the music. I know the song. It is Merle Haggard's *Strangers*.

There is another sound in the night: the cackling of men, laughing wickedly, enjoying themselves in the room down below.

I am breathing very hard now. I am breathing hard and I am shaking and I am not sure what to do.

I look back at the mesquite scrub behind the house but I do not see the thing in white there. I realize I do not see him there because that is not where he is.

I know where he is. I know that he is waiting for me.

I turn back and stare at the golden light pouring into the dark parking lot. I do not want to go, but I know he has Bear. He has had him all this time, perhaps. We have lived in his shadow for so long, but Bear has dwelled deeper in that darkness than I, so he is lost now, and I must bring him back.

I walk down the hill, gripping my flashlight, trying to ignore the terror clawing at the back of my mind.

I am level with the motel now. I can hear the voices in the room beyond saying things, shouting things, rough, guttural cries of encouragement.

"Get it off her! Pop 'em out and let's see 'em..."

"There you go! Turn around, hon! Spin around!"

"Beautiful! A thoroughbred of a girl, I got to say."

The distance to the room feels agonizing. I keep going. I am very close to the corner of the motel now, looking along one leg of the U at the room. I still cannot see within it. If I walked to the center of the motel I could, but I do not want them to see me. Or perhaps I do not wish to see what awaits.

"Where you get these from, Corbin? Where you get these girls from?"

"Bend her over! Prove it! Prove it, boy!"

Then a burst of whoops and cries and cackling. I press my back to the wall and inch down toward the room. The music is so loud now, with a scratchy quality, and I know somehow it has to be playing on an old record player, some old thing from decades long ago, and I smell the whisky and the beer and the cigarette smoke as I get closer, and I hear the whoops and cackling of the men, and I get the overwhelming feeling that I am glimpsing some wound in the time of this place, a festering injury of something that occurred here long ago, or occurred many times, and maybe it's still happening, maybe it's happening over and over and over again, over and over and over again like the world itself cannot forget.

I am just next to the room now, my back still pressed to the cinderblock wall, my eyes fixed on the stream of light spilling onto the parking lot before me, and the shadows of the men within, milling about, watching something occur, some horrid violation, some abuse I don't wish to see, but I know I must because I know he has Bear, I know he does, I just know he does.

Has he always had Bear? Always had me? I do not know.

I take a breath, and brace myself to pivot around and look.

But before I move the light goes out, and the music dies.

All is silent, all is dark.

I stand next to the windows of the room, bewildered and terrified, not breathing.

Did they know? Did he flee my approach? Is it over?

I don't know. But I know I must find Bear and get out of here, get away from this poisoned place, get us free and find somewhere clear.

I take another breath, then wheel out and stare into the room with the hatch.

The door is open. The room within is pitch black.

I stare into the darkness, then flick on my flashlight and shine it within.

Bear is standing before the open panel of flooring with his back to me, the metal of the closed hatch glinting in the light. His shadow dances on the blank wall ahead of him. His hands are at his sides. He is perfectly still. The room is as I have always known it, unadorned and simple.

"Bear?" I whisper.

Then something lurches in the shadows before him, in the corner of the room.

There is someone else in there with him. A huge, hulking man-shaped figure, adorned in white.

Then the whole world is screaming. My brother whirls around, his eyes wide and wild, and he is screaming at me, advancing on me, howling like an animal. I have never heard a human being make such a sound in my life.

I fall backwards and drop the flashlight, and my back strikes the asphalt of the parking lot, but my brother is advancing on me, screaming and howling and shrieking.

"Try to take it away?" he is screaming. *"Sell it and take it away? Sell it and take it away, take it away?"*

He emerges from the door of the room, his hands in fists, spittle flying from his lips, and I scoot backward, terrified.

Yet as he exits something else follows him, ducking out the door. Something tall and broad, watching me, its face obscured in shadow. It begins circling us, observing what Bear does to me.

He kicks me in the side, and I gasp and curl up. Then he grabs me by my shirt front and begins pummeling me, striking me again and again and again, and I feel my lip split and my cheek burst and my eardrum pop and my eyes fill with blood, and he keeps screaming, he just keeps screaming, screaming as he beats me, screaming as the world goes numb and I stare up at the night sky and all I see is the man-thing in white slowly shuffling forward, its eyes wet little glints lurking at the back of its skull, its hands gleaming with blood, its broad flesh shuddering in the light of the stars, and then all the world is lost and silent.

THEN COME THE SOFT MOMENTS, the dark moments, sensations of being moved, of the taste of dust and blood.

I awake with my head bent forward and screams echoing in my ears.

"Try to ruin it!" my brother is ranting. "Try to ruin it all. After I worked so hard, so hard, so hard. Try to ruin it all, to ruin what I'm owed."

My mind is little more than a bleary smear running through my skull and my eyes are near swollen shut and my mouth is full of blood. I try to lift my head but my neck screams in pain, and I wince and gather myself before finally cracking an eye and peering around.

I am in our living room, in the place where I slashed through the floor. I am bound to a chair, the ropes biting into the flesh around my wrists, and my brother is pacing around me, holding his pistol, raving and swearing.

"All this work," he says. "Take it away. Lose this. Son of a bitch. Fuck. Fuck! Son of a bitch. Son of a bitch! Fuck! Fuck! Fuck this! Fuck them! Fuck this!"

I stare at him, hissing swears and pacing madly, and I realize I have seen this before.

I saw this when I was a child. It is one of the few memories I have of my father.

Yet I see we are not alone. For he is there, beyond the sliding glass door, bloated and pale and still, standing in the trees with the moon just behind his head. He watches Bear so closely, so greedily, his face lost in shadow but his eyes gleaming queerly.

"Bear," I whisper.

Bear whirls around, spitting and screaming. "Don't you dare talk! Don't you dare talk! Don't you dare talk to me! You want to ruin all this! You want to ruin what's owed to me!"

He points the gun at my skull, and I shut my eyes and feel my crotch flood with hot urine. Then he whirls away again, slapping at his forehead with his other hand, hitting himself once, twice, three times, swearing and cursing and ranting like a madman.

"Bear," I say. "This is not you."

"I got nothing!" he screams at me. "I have *nothing!*"

"Bear."

"I was supposed to have so much more! I was supposed to be so much more! I was supposed to be so much more!"

I realize now that I know the way that Bear has combed his hair. That curious, old-fashioned look. I realize I saw it once before, in a picture of a big man standing beside his wife, he in a white crew-neck T-shirt and slacks, she small and frail and delicate.

The thing in white steps closer to the sliding glass door, shuddering queerly.

"Bear," I say. "It's him. He's here. Corbin is here. He's putting all this inside you. He's still hungry. He still wants to do the things he's always done."

"Don't you fucking talk!" Bear shrieks at me. "Don't you fucking talk! You're like all the others! You're just like all the others!"

"The things you've done," I say. "The things you want. Listen to me. They're not things you really want. They're things *he* wants. Things he wants to do, so he's using you."

"It wasn't supposed to be like this," he weeps. "A house. A wife. A job. A home."

"You can still have that," I say. "We both can."

"I can't," he says. "Not now. It's all changed so much. A man can't get what's owed to him. All that's left is for him to take it."

"That's Corbin in you, in your head," I say. "That's him putting that in your mind."

"It isn't, though," he sobs. "It isn't."

Bear faces away from me, head bowed, and sobs, pistol still clutched in his hand.

"Is she still alive?" I ask.

He doesn't answer.

"The girl," I say. "The missing girl. Is she still alive, Bear?"

The thing in white is very close now, standing at the glass of the door, eyes gleaming like a cat's catching the light.

"How long have you had her?" I ask. "How long have you hidden her from me?"

"I just wanted a place where I could feel like a man," says Bear. "A place to live as I choose. A place to be free."

"Bear," I say.

He turns and raises his pistol and points it at me, at my skull, and I brace myself but I look into his face, his eyes.

Despite everything, it is still the face of the child I knew. The child who in the long and whimpering nights would explore my body for wounds and count my teeth and get me ice to suck on when I had a split lip, and hold me until I fell asleep in his twin bed with him.

"Bear," I say.

Something crumples in his face. Then he raises the pistol and brings it down on me, and the world quivers and shakes and he is lost.

I DO NOT KNOW HOW long I stay bound to the chair. It feels like an eternity. Perhaps it is an eternity.

Then I smell alcohol. I smell rubbing alcohol, and cleaning agents.

Then my mind fills with the bleak white fluorescent lights of the hospital in Abilene, so long ago.

And I suddenly I am there. I am there, and I am five years old again and my aunt is walking down the hall with me, my little hand clutching hers, hers so soft and wrinkly and the nails so carefully painted, and I don't know why I'm there but I know it must be bad, it must be really bad, everyone is acting like it's really bad, there are adults there and they're all talking the way adults talk when they don't want children to hear, and I wish Bear was there with me, I wish my brother were here.

But then I see he is. I see Bear is there, seated at the end of a row of chairs in the hospital waiting room, his skinny legs dangling off the chair, his hands in his lap, his head bowed as the adults fuss and talk around him. One of them is a sheriff, and this disturbs me. I have seen many police before and they are always only there when something has gone so bad with Papa and Momma.

My aunt gives my hand a tug and tells me to go and sit next to my brother. It has been a long time since I have seen him, a long time since they pulled me out and left him there. I am worried he has forgotten me, because he does not look up when I approach.

"Bear?" I say as I come close.

He blinks, and slowly looks up. And somehow when I look into his eyes I know that something is broken in my brother. That finally Papa found something to break inside him that was worse than a lip or a finger or a rib. Something hidden and fragile and irreplaceable, something that could never be put right, put back.

"She's gone," he says to me. "She's gone." Then there is a pause, and he says, "No. That's not it. She's not just gone. He killed her. That's what he did."

I don't understand what he means. But I sit next to him, and I mimic his pose: I let my legs dangle, and I put my hands in my lap, and I bow my head. Two little lost boys, adrift in the shadows of things they do not understand.

Somewhere in the room I hear my aunt sigh, and whisper, "The things these men do."

I AWAKE TO THE SOUND of tapping.

I sit up, my head aching and pounding. I feel sick, nauseous. I am probably concussed.

I see I am still bound to the chair in the house. It is still night. I am alone.

But then there is another tap, at the glass back door.

I look at the door. There is no one there. But then another tap—and then a pop as the glass door opens, and begins to slide away.

I watch the door as it opens, the pale light of the moon streaming through the glass.

There is no one opening the door. It is as if it is opening of its own accord.

As I watch, the glass door slowly slides to a stop. The wind blows through the gap, making the dust twirl and dance across the floor and the carpet. I stare at the open door and I suddenly feel so cold, like my very bones were wrought of ice.

Then I see them: impressions in the carpet, appearing one after the other. Like someone invisible is slowly walking to me, in from the open door.

I begin to tremble as the footsteps grow closer and closer, until they are just before me. And then I hear a whisper in the dark—a woman's voice, soft and hushed.

"*Él no está aquí. Se fue a ver lo que el hombre le hace a la niña.*"

I stare into the darkness, bewildered and terrified. Then I feel a tug at my hands, once, twice, and the ropes fall away.

I stare at my hands, trembling before my face. The iciness in the air seems to grow, and I feel whatever is in here with me shifting, moving away, moving toward the door. I untie the bonds at my feet and hurry after, unsure where I am going or what I will see.

Once outside I stand on the porch, staring out at the mesquite trees, the moon high and bright and thick and the only sound the wind.

Then I spy the old metal roof in the far corner of the lot, nearly a quarter of a mile away.

A voice on the wind, soft and sad.

"Mi bebé. Mi bebé está ahí."

I listen for a moment. Then I start off into the scrub.

I ENTER THE LINE OF trees. At some point it feels like I cross some threshold, and it is as if a cloud or veil is cast over the moon, and the whole nightscape becomes blue and gray and inverted, a warping of this world, or perhaps a shadow-version of what I know.

Then I see faces in the trees, watching me, observing my procession toward the shed with expressions both sad and eager.

They are all girls, all lost in this place, none older than twenty or thirty. As I pass they point to the shed and whisper, again and again and again.

"Estoy ahí."

"Ahí es donde me puso. Ahí es donde me acuesto."

"Mis bebés están ahí. Mis gemelos. Están allí."

I keep walking. I walk through the dreamy night as the fronds of the mesquite trees brush my face and the soft red earth crunches underfoot until finally I come to the old wooden shack with the tin roof.

I stand before the door. It is locked with a padlock, but the wood is old. I pry it away easily, even in my weakened state, and I look inside.

The shack is empty except for a few tools: shovels, rakes, and so on.

But I know better now. I know Corbin Pugh liked to put his secrets underground.

I dig at the earthen floor of the shack with one of the shovels and soon I find something, just inches below the surface. It is an oil drum, and after digging some more I find a second, and a third, all buried here in the dry red earth. I stand there in the shack, staring at old oil drums, and then I use the point of the spade as a crowbar and pry open one of the drums.

The lid falls away. The smell of rot and putrefaction is heavy even now, and the light of the moon slices through the gaps in the wood of the shack to outline the jumble of bones below, the nest of tibias and vertebrae, and skulls.

Or what is left of the skulls. For so many are fractured, and smashed.

And some of the skulls are so very, very small.

I wish to scream. I wish to scream and howl and claw my eyes in dismay, in despair, in misery. But I know I cannot. I cannot alert the thing that stalks this place, to let it know what I have found.

For I know his other secret now. I know what is in the hatch.

I kneel over the open barrel and stare in at the remains of these women, these girls, these children, these infants. Perhaps some were brought here by foolishness or a mistake or desperation, and perhaps some were brought here by force or lies; and still others, I know, were simply born into this place through no will or choice of their own, born into this desolate stretch of earth to take but a handful of breaths before their lives were snatched away, castoffs of a bondage that had no interest in reparations for its consequences.

I think of what was bought with these lives, with this blood. What appetites they slaked. What humiliations they had to endure and still endure, sealed in barrels in an indifferent pile, their memories lost here at the edge of God's creation.

And I decide there will be no more. There will be no more of this.

I turn around and begin to trudge through the trees. As I near the house I spy a new face watching me from among the branches, a waifish woman with large eyes and a wide mouth and a curiously square upper lip. Her straight brown hair is parted down the middle.

Our eyes meet. She is so sad, so lost. I know that she has waited here the longest.

"I'll stop him," I say. "I will. I promise I will."

She says nothing. I continue on into the house. I find my cell phone and I call the police and tell them to come quick. I don't stay on the line and I don't bother to say more because I know the thing that's here won't give me time, not enough to stop what's going to happen.

I go to Bear's room but I do not find his shotgun or pistol. He must have taken them. I go to my room and I dig in the closet until I find the ball-peen hammer.

As I leave the house I stop and look back at the living room, and the one picture hanging on the wall.

An old print depicting the battle of San Jacinto, and below it the name and the date: 1836.

I WALK DOWN TO THE motel like a drunk, stumbling through the earth, through the handfuls of brush around the road. My head is swimming and my belly is sick but I walk on, I keep walking, the hammer clenched tight in my hand.

There is no light on in the room with the hatch. But I know he is not in the room now. He is beneath it.

I walk to the room with the hatch and look inside, and I see the linoleum floor is open but the hatch is closed. I walk in and listen.

There is not a sound. But there wouldn't be, I realize. Corbin would have made it soundproof.

I grip the hammer tight in my hand. With the other I spin the tumblers on the lock to 1836. Then I grasp the handle, twist, and pull up.

As the hatch opens there is a tremendous eruption of music, Merle Haggard blaring so loud it makes me recoil, and there is a stink as well, the stale scent of urine and feces, like a rodent's nest. Below the hatch door is a short set of ladder rungs leading to a cavity below, which is lit with a dull yellow light.

I recognize the light. It is one of our battery-powered lamps, for the rare times that we worked on the motel at night.

I look down into the cavity below. It is like a cellar or a bunker, tall enough for a person to stand up in.

I cannot see anyone below. But I know.

Before I climb down into the bunker I look at the open side of the hatch door. It is metal but it has been clawed at and scratched at and struck countless times, and here and there it is streaked with blood from when someone clawed at it so much their nails or very fingers broke.

I swallow and descend into the bunker, hammer clenched in my hand.

The bunker is larger than I'd imagined, nearly thirty feet by thirty feet and seven feet tall. The battery lamp is on the floor at the far end, and it is there that I see them.

Bear sits on the ground next to the lamp, his back against the wall. He is shirtless. The shotgun and pistol lie beside him on the ground. On his other side is a record player, which is playing Merle Haggard.

Beyond him is a chair. Tied to the chair, just as I was tied to the chair above, is a girl of about nineteen. She is weeping, and filthy, and thin and dehydrated, with a gag stuffed into her mouth. I can see from here that her lips are bright pink. Her nose is bloodied and empty chip bags and jugs of water sit about the base of the chair.

Urine is pooled around her feet. It is clear she has been here for days. She looks at me as I climb down the ladder. Her eyes go wide, but she is either smart enough or so exhausted that she does not scream.

How long has she been here, I wonder? Since Houston? Before?

Was Bear truly skilled enough to conceal her? Or was I so lost that I missed the signs? Or was it something else? Did Corbin Pugh cast a smoke over my mind so I could not see what was right before me?

I study the scene. I do not see the thing in white. I do not see Corbin Pugh stalking this chamber. But I know he is here. I know this is the secret heart of this place, and who he is.

I slowly begin to approach Bear, the hammer in my hand. I look at the walls. They are bloody and scratched, likely from some woman or girl or child who went mad here in the darkness.

"Got to take back what's yours," whispers Bear as I approach.

I slow, but I do not stop.

"I wanted a place of my own," he whispers. "A place free from all what's out there. All that happened to me. All that's in me. But he tricked me."

"I know," I say.

"I'm not free in here," he says. "I'm trapped. Still trapped. Out from the memory of one man and into another."

"I know, Bear."

I'm fifteen feet away from him now. I eye the guns on the ground. Bear does not seem to be making a move for them.

"I know you know," says Bear. He reaches out and turns the lantern down. "But you also know he ain't ever going to let me go. Nor you. Not now."

And it is then that I feel him. I feel him pacing the room in the dark, walking about the puddle of light on the floor, this tremendous, hulking thing, watching me and shuddering in the shadows.

The girl in the chair whimpers.

"You're not like him," I say to Bear.

"I am," says Bear. "Look at me."

"He kept girls down here. He did horrible things to them here, Bear, and when they were dead he buried them in the shack up there and their families never knew what happened to them."

I walk closer to Bear, watching him sitting against the wall, his head bowed.

"You are not like that," I say. "You are not like him, Bear Pugh."

"No," he whispers. "But I'm still a Pugh. And it's like you said. It's like lead. You drink it and it gets in you and you can never get it out."

I take another step.

"They pulled you out," he says. "You only drank a little. But I drank a lot."

The thing in the dark keeps pacing around us. I'm very close now.

Then something hardens in Bear's face.

"I can't end this," he says. "I never could. But you can."

"Bear, no," I say.

He shifts forward, reaching for the shotgun. "Just do it."

He stands and turns and lifts the shotgun, pointing it at the girl in the chair. She screams through her gag.

I can tell he is going to do it. The thing in white pauses in its pacing, watching greedily.

I move without even thinking. I feel the hammer leap in my hand as it strikes the back of my brother's head. There is the crash of the shotgun as he falls, and the burst of heat and smoke and dust, and the scream of the girl, and my bloodied ears fill with a tinnitus whine.

I am standing there in the smoke, the light from the lantern smeared through the dust about me, and my brother is at my feet and my bruised brain is spinning.

Then I see him approach me.

He slides through the smoke, through the dust, huge and broad and pale, his eyes little more than sparks in the shadows of his face.

She could be yours.

I hear the girl screaming nearby. She is little more than a silhouette in the smoke.

You're all alone here. Free from responsibilities. Free from consequence.

I stare at the thing in white. He peers down on me with his little muddy eyes.

A place where you can have what you deserve. What is owed to you. What is owed to a man. Is that not where you most want to be?

I try not to listen. I try. But I am suddenly overcome with the urge, the desire to go back to the ladder and shut the hatch and then rip the girl out of this chair and press her against the floor of this place and listen to her whimper as I have my way with her, as I humiliate her, as I degrade her, as I inflict my being upon hers.

I shut my eyes.

I see within my mind a woman standing on a sidewalk, a child on her hip, watching me leave.

"No," I whisper. "That's not where I want to be at all."

112

I fumble forward blindly. I have to keep my eyes shut, I realize. I cannot see him. Cannot perceive him. Cannot get more of his poison inside me.

I walk forward until I find the girl, and my fingers trail down her back until I find her bonds. I untie them and I untie her hands and then she must have removed her gag because she is sobbing then, sobbing and screaming hysterically.

"Let's go," I say. "Let's go now. The police are coming. Let's go now."

Blindly I lead her away from the chair, away from that place, away from that thing in white, and back to the ladder, back to the surface, back to the motel, where the horizon is strobing with blue and red lights, and the night sky is full of sirens.

Then I kneel and lay my head against the bare floor and shut my eyes and I am gone.

I AWAKE. I AM IN a hospital bed.

They tell me I have a severe concussion. They tell me I have been arrested. They tell me I have been arrested as an accomplice in the kidnap and rape and attempted murder of Judith Scald.

I take this information indifferently. The world is still very distant and muted to me. All is so unreal.

I whisper to them. I tell them to search the corner of the yard. Search the shack. Find the women there. Find the women and the babies.

I sleep again.

I AWAKE. I AM STILL in a hospital bed. There are people around me. They tell me I am no longer charged as an accomplice in the kidnap and rape and attempted murder of Judith Scald.

Again, I take this information indifferently. I do not know how to feel anymore. I have forgotten such a thing. It does not matter anymore.

A day passes. Perhaps more. Then Sheriff Corddry comes, accompanied by many other police officers, all of them very angry looking, and they all crowd around my hospital bed and ask me many questions.

I come to understand that they have found Shauna, and questioned her, and she has given them her story, which somewhat exonerates me. And the girl—this Judith Scald—has repeatedly and emphatically testified that I was not complicit in what happened to her. They have checked the dates and confirmed I was in Houston when she was kidnapped, and that it was all Bear—Bear and one other person.

Someone big, who lived in the chamber below the motel.

"Who's the second man?" the sheriff asks me. "Who was down there with her?"

"Corbin Pugh," I say.

"Corbin Pugh is dead," the sheriff says.

"How many women were buried in the oil drums in the yard?" I ask.

The sheriff studies me coldly. "Nine."

"And babies?"

The coldness grows. "Three."

I shut my eyes, and weep. I weep, for that is all I can do, so I weep until there are no more tears within me.

SHERIFF CORDDRY NEVER STOPS SUSPECTING me. Even after all the other officers have gone, he still questions me. Again and again, he asks if I knew about the girls buried in the yard. Did I come to Coahora for that? Did I know? How did I know? Was it a family secret? Are we a cult?

I do not tell him the truth. I know he would not believe me. So I tell him that that Bear found out about the burial in the yard, and what his grand-uncle had done in that place, and the discovery drove Bear mad.

This is somewhat true. Bear did find something under the Moon and Stars. And it did drive him mad.

"Are their families being found and notified?" I ask.

"Whose?" says Corddry.

"The women. The girls buried in the yard. Their families must have been looking for them. They must have been looking for their daughters and sisters."

"Why do you care?"

"Why wouldn't I?"

There is a moment of silence. I understand that the sheriff despises me not because he truly believes I took part in this, but because I have made him look foolish. I found the girl and I found the bodies and it was all right there for him to find, if only he'd gone looking.

"Did you find his wife?" I ask. "Buried there in the yard?"

"We don't know. We're looking."

"She's there," I say. "She must be. And the children there…"

"Yeah?"

"I think they're Corbin's."

He stares at me. "He murdered his own babies?"

"I think so."

"Why in the hell would he do that?"

"Because he didn't want a family. He didn't want to be burdened. He wanted to be free."

"You people," says Corddry, disgusted. He begins to stand. "You come in here and you stir it all up and make us all look bad."

"What was it you said, sheriff?" I say. "Every town needs a place where people can go to put a toe out of line? Would you have ever gone looking for those girls? If the

Moon and Stars were still operating, would you have ever gone looking for them? Or would you prefer to imagine that boys will just be boys, and sweep it all away?"

He stares at me, furious, puts his hat on, and walks out.

EVENTUALLY THEY LET ME SEE him. They let me get out of my hospital bed and I hobble down the hall to the room where he lies.

Where he is guarded. Where he breathes, and his heart beats, but he does not live.

I look upon my brother, lying in the hospital bed, his head bandaged, his eyes closed. How small and diminished he looks in the dull fluorescent lights of this place.

All the tubes running in and out of him. All the beeping, the alarms, the nurses coming in to change bandages and drain this or that.

"Can I touch him?" I ask the police officer.

The officer makes a face and nods.

I limp over to Bear in my hospital gown. I take his hand and look at him, tied to the bed, his mind failing in his skull, his body full of tubes.

"Hey, Bear," I say softly.

He does not respond. My ears ring with the chirrups of the countless machines.

"We're like castaways, aren't we, Bear," I say softly. "Washing up on a strange shore with no idea how to work in this world. We never had a blueprint to follow. No instructions, no guide. Nothing but wrecks and ruins."

The slow suck of air as a pump winds up and down. A muttering of voices from some distant room. How small and reduced he seems, as if some secret part of him has been invisibly amputated.

"It hurts," I said. "It's always hurt. But I thought talking about hurt was something I wasn't allowed to do. But I wished I'd talked with you. I wished we'd talked. I'm sorry I wasn't there before. But I'm here now, Bear."

I watch him, still and dull and silent in the bed. I know he will not live much longer. I know I will be the only one here for him, in the end.

He has no one else. There is no one else, for those who grew up in the shadows of such men.

So I sit with him, and wait. And once he has found his final rest I know I will go home. I will go home to those people to whom I owe so much, to the wife and child who deserve so much more from me. And I know I still will not understand how to be the thing they need me to be.

But I will ask them. I will ask them for help, to show me how to give, for I want to learn. And once I know, I will never stop giving.

TO TRAVEL ACROSS WEST TEXAS at night is to pass through bursts of bright and seas of shadow. It is to travel across a place of tremendous opposites and inverses: of stillness and movement, of frozen landscapes and churning highways, of empty wilderness and crowded crossroads, of vast darknesses and fluttering flares.

To travel across west Texas at night is to play with a dangerous dream, the dream many men toy with. A dream of finding some blank stretch of forgotten earth unscrolling beneath the heavens and thinking, how can I make this mine, and what shall I do here, what shall I do with this kingdom of my own. And what they write there with their hearts upon the empty page of creation ought be forgotten.